WHERE THE DROWNED GIRLS GO

ALSO BY SEANAN McGUIRE

Middlegame
Dusk or Dark or Dawn or Day
Sparrow Hill Road
The Girl in the Green Silk Gown
Angel of the Overpass
Deadlands: Boneyard

THE WAYWARD CHILDREN SERIES
Every Heart a Doorway
Down Among the Sticks and Bones
Beneath the Sugar Sky
In an Absent Dream
Come Tumbling Down
Across the Green Grass Fields
Where the Drowned Girls Go

THE OCTOBER DAYE SERIES
Rosemary and Rue
A Local Habitation
An Artificial Night
Late Eclipses
One Salt Sea
Ashes of Honor
Chimes at Midnight
The Winter Long
A Red-Rose Chain
Once Broken Faith
The Brightest Fell
Night and Silence
The Unkindest Tide
A Killing Frost
When Sorrows Come

THE INCRYPTID SERIES
Discount Armageddon
Midnight Blue-Light Special
Half-Off Ragnarok
Pocket Apocalypse
Chaos Choreography
Magic for Nothing
Tricks for Free

That Ain't Witchcraft
Imaginary Numbers
Calculated Risks

THE INDEXING SERIES
Indexing
Indexing: Reflections

COLLECTIONS
Laughter at the Academy
Dying with Her Cheer Pants On:
  Stories of the Fighting Pumpkins
Letters to the Pumpkin King

AS MIRA GRANT

THE NEWSFLESH SERIES
Feed
Deadline
Blackout
Feedback
Rise: The Complete Newsflesh
  Collection (short stories)

THE PARASITOLOGY SERIES
Parasite
Symbiont
Chimera

Rolling in the Deep
Into the Drowning Deep

Final Girls
Kingdom of Needle and Bone
In the Shadow of Spindrift House
Square[3]
Alien: Echo

AS A. DEBORAH BAKER

THE UP-AND-UNDER SERIES
Over the Woodward Wall
Along the Saltwise Sea

WHERE THE DROWNED GIRLS GO

SEANAN McGUIRE

A TOM DOHERTY ASSOCIATES BOOK

NEW YORK

WHERE THE DROWNED GIRLS GO

Copyright © 2021 by Seanan McGuire

Interior art copyright © 2021 by Rovina Cai

All rights reserved.

Edited by Lee Harris

A Tordotcom Book
Published by Tom Doherty Associates
120 Broadway
New York, NY 10271

www.tor.com

Tor® is a registered trademark of Macmillan Publishing Group, LLC.

Library of Congress Cataloging-in-Publication Data

Names: McGuire, Seanan, author.
Title: Where the drowned girls go / Seanan McGuire.
Description: First edition. | New York : Tordotcom, a
Tom Doherty Associates Book, 2022. | Series: Wayward children ; 7
Identifiers: LCCN 2021033095 (print) | LCCN 2021033096 (ebook) |
ISBN 9781250213624 (hardcover) | ISBN 9781250213617 (ebook)
Classification: LCC PS3607.R36395 W54 2022 (print) |
LCC PS3607.R36395 (ebook) | DDC 813/.6—dc23
LC record available at https://lccn.loc.gov/2021033095
LC ebook record available at https://lccn.loc.gov/2021033096

Our books may be purchased in bulk for promotional,
educational, or business use. Please contact your local bookseller
or the Macmillan Corporate and Premium Sales Department
at 1-800-221-7945, extension 5442, or by email at
MacmillanSpecialMarkets@macmillan.com.

First Edition: January 2022

Printed in the United States of America

0 9 8 7 6 5 4 3 2 1

FOR ALL MY MERMAIDS.
NO MATTER WHERE YOU WEAR YOUR SCALES,
I SEE YOU.

PART I

BEHIND CLOSED DOORS

HOME AGAIN

CHILDREN HAVE ALWAYS BEEN drawn to the doors.

Scholars have recorded the adventures of the travelers, those whose lost and lonely yearnings were strong enough to attract the attention of something greater than themselves, for centuries. Those stories can be seen in myth and legend, in fairy tale and folk song, from across the world. The boy who spent a night in a mushroom ring and woke to find his baby sister's grandchildren occupying the family farm; the girl who tumbled down a well and lived for a century in the halls of a Dragon King before touching the wrong trinket and finding herself cast back into the mud, rendered an exile in her own homeland. It can be difficult to find the places where fiction ends and fact begins, but perhaps that's simply a part of the process of traveling, of visiting places where the customs and cultures and laws of physical reality are different than they are here.

Not all children who find their door come back. Some are so sure of the rightness of their journeys, are so bone-deep and unshakable in their convictions, that they never go through the trials of being forced to choose where they'll grow up. Others fall prey to the myriad dangers that lurk in worlds built on foundations of stone and story. Their graves are forgotten, or tended with the reverence afforded to heroes, or shunned with the fear and suspicion afforded to monsters, but they all have one thing in common: they're graves. The bodies they conceal have found their endings. Their stories are over.

Mostly. There are worlds where death itself is malleable, where anything can be rewritten, be undone, if the right approach is taken. Worlds where the air bleeds words and lightning can rewrite the past. Worlds where things can be taken back.

But taking something back doesn't mean it never happened, only that someone was willing to fight hard enough to change it. Some graves lie empty; some children run home. Some children hide under their covers and cry, not for the beauty of a sky filled with rainbows or a field of singing roses, but from the weight of all they've seen and done and lost and paid.

Not all children who come back find peace in the memory of their journeys. Some children find themselves walking in the broken spaces of their own experience, unable to untangle who they were from who they've become, unable to find their way fully home.

Still lost. Still lonely. But now without even a door to guide them.

When Eleanor West had decided to open her school, her sanctuary, her Home for Wayward Children, she had known from the beginning that there would be children she couldn't save. Children whose journeys had broken them in ways she was unequipped to handle; children whose parents refused to understand the difference between harming them and healing them. Still, she had looked at her probable losses with open eyes, and decided that the cost was worth it. Still, she had placed the sign in the window, and hoped it would be enough to guide them home, to harbor, to her.

No solicitation. No visitors.

No quests.

1 SO MANY WAYS TO DROWN

CORA MILLER WOKE WITH a start in a room that was still dark, drenched in the moonlight coming through the window, with the sound of screams ringing in her ears. She sat up in bed, her heart pounding, and tried to catch her breath, waiting for the moment when her roommate would demand to know why she'd been screaming *again*, wasn't she tired of waking up terrified every night, didn't she think it was time to talk to the school's new therapist?

But the new therapist—a very nice woman named Nichole, who had moved into the office that used to belong to Katherine Lundy, hanging her diplomas on the walls alongside cheerful motivational posters and pictures of her dogs—had gone through her door more than thirty years ago, and had come home with a head stuffed full of pleasant memories and happy dreams. She believed that it was possible to move beyond the doors, to grow into someone who could be happy in *this* world forever, forsaking all others. Based on what she'd told the students, nothing on the other side of her door had been malicious, or malevolent, or made of teeth.

No, Cora didn't want to talk to Nichole. Didn't want to sit down with a pleasantly smiling woman in a pleasantly decorated office and listen to her tell pleasantly couched lies about how things were going to get better. Things weren't going to get better. Maybe not ever.

Antoinette didn't say anything. She was still dead to the

world, one arm flung over her face to block the watery moonlight, her hair spread out across her pillow like a riot of coral fronds. The moon could tint everything in silver, could wash the world in white, but it couldn't steal the foxfire brightness from Antsy's hair. Sometimes Cora wondered if Antsy's hair was the reason Eleanor had decided they should share a room. "If you have two girls with unrealistically brightly colored hair, let them clog up the same bathtub drain" seemed like the sort of logic Eleanor liked to trade in.

It wasn't like they had very much else in common. Cora had traveled to the Trenches, an underwater world full of mermaids, mysteries, and maritime monsters. Her door had opened when she tried to take her own life, unable to endure one more day of the constant judgmental mockery of the people who were supposed to be her peers, and just when she'd been finding her fins in the deeps, a whirlpool had swept her back into the life she had never expected to return to.

Antoinette had traveled to a Nonsense world, and a dry one at that, a place of jumbled boxes and endless shelves, where all the lost things went. "I got lost, and so I went where the lost things go" was how she had explained it, as matter-of-factly as if nothing could have possibly made more sense. She was fickle and fractious, and would have made a better roommate for Sumi. Only Sumi wasn't required to have a roommate anymore, since apparently the rules were different for people who had died and come back.

It wasn't fair, but what about the world really was? The jagged lines of her latest nightmare were still lingering, not expunged by screaming as they would normally have been; they cast strange shadows in the corners of the room, shadows that moved and twisted and bent, like the tentacled arms of some great, terrible—

Cora shuddered and pulled her eyes away from the wall, swiping her hands across them in short, furious motions, like nightmares were just another bit of grit that could be wiped away. At least with the lights down, she couldn't see her own skin; couldn't see the thin scrim of oil-slick iridescence that covered every inch of her, and had since she danced with the Drowned Gods in the waters of the Moors.

She swung her legs around to plant her feet on the floor, finally admitting that sleep was finished for the night: sleep was over and done. Maybe she could catch a nap in the early afternoon, when the sun was thick and buttery, and even the deepest shadows were easy to see through.

Antoinette still didn't stir. Cora took a moment to breathe and look at her roommate, waiting for her heart to settle in her chest. She used to be able to sleep like that. She used to put her head down on the pillow and let the night take her away, off into dreams full of deep, diamond-dappled water, diving down where the currents were warm and the waters were always welcoming.

Since the Moors, though . . . since the Moors, her dreams were still full of water and waves, but the sea she swam in while she slept was no longer remotely kind. It was filled with teeth, and colder than she would have believed the water could be. Worst of all were the whispers, which moved with the tide and promised her anything she wanted—promised her the world's oceans, promised to return her fins and scales and free her from the bonds of gravity, if she would just stop trying so hard to swim away from them. All they wanted was to love her. All they needed her to do was turn around and let them in.

The halls of the school were empty at this hour. If Christopher was awake, he would be wandering in the trees behind the building, playing his flute for the small midnight creatures that moved among the roots, hoping not to be seen. He was the only quasi-nocturnal student currently in residence, with Nancy having gone back to the Halls of the Dead and Jack at home in the Moors. It made the school feel a little darker at night, knowing that everyone else was sleeping.

Cora's tenure at Eleanor West's Home for Wayward Children hadn't overlapped with Nancy or the Wolcott twins, but her shadows hadn't always been so tangled, or so tempting. She used to sleep through the night. She used to be fine with solitude on the rare evenings when she couldn't.

She walked along the hall as quietly as possible, wincing every time a floorboard creaked or the foundation made a small, settling groan, waiting for one of the doors lining the hall to slam open and reveal one of her fellow students, disheveled and angry at being woken from a sound night's sleep. If that happened, she wasn't sure she'd be able to stop herself from slapping someone and waking the rest of the hall as she screamed, "So you got woken up *once*. So what? I haven't slept through the night in *months*!"

But no doors opened. The halls remained empty, and the classrooms she passed on her way to the bathroom were the same, their doors standing open and the blinds pulled down over their windows. All those rooms would be full soon enough, packed with students who didn't necessarily want to learn, but who didn't want to spend all their time sitting quietly and waiting for the world to shift under their feet. They'd been lucky enough to see the world change once. Most of them wouldn't be lucky enough to see it change again.

And even if they did, luck wasn't always good.

Cora shivered as she walked along the hall. Kade had his Compass, his little map to all the different worlds represented by the student body, but it wasn't accurate. It could never be accurate. Worlds could be oriented in different directions but still be very, very similar to one another. Drowned Worlds were Drowned Worlds, regardless of whether or not they had Logical rules or leaned toward the Wicked. A direction wasn't a description, it was just a set of . . . of fundamental rules. Saying that any two people who'd traveled in the same direction had to get along was like saying that two people who'd experienced the same kind of gravity as children had to be the best-of bestest best friends.

According to Kade's map, the Trenches were a Logical, Wicked world, but Cora had never been able to see the Wickedness in them. They weren't cruel. The currents could be harsh and almost random, but if you stayed with your shoal and avoided dangerous waters, you could potentially swim forever without meeting anything that wanted to harm you. According to that same map, the Moors were also Logical and Wicked, and Cora couldn't stand the thought of her kind, beloved home having anything in common with that nightmare landscape, with that leering red moon washed in so much blood that it would never be clean again, with those deep and dangerous waters.

Thinking of the waters of the Moors was enough to trigger another cascade of whispers from the dark. Cora shuddered and walked faster. Eleanor and Kade both said that the Drowned Gods couldn't reach her here, couldn't slide their tentacles across the gulf between worlds to wrap around her ankles and drag her under, but she knew they were wrong, because she heard them constantly. They haunted her. And everyone knew that things from the other side of the door could absolutely leak through into this reality. Her hair had been brown, not aquamarine, before she found her fins. Christopher would die without his flute—literally die. Seraphina was the kind of beautiful that stopped hearts, and everyone who'd seen pictures of her from before her travels said that she hadn't always been like that. She'd been attractive, not impossible. The doors made changes. The doors stayed with you.

If her hair could keep growing in blue as the depths of the ocean, if Seraphina could still walk through life in a perfumed cloud of her own grace, who was to say that the Drowned Gods couldn't reach through whatever gap allowed those things to happen? Who was to say they couldn't claim what they already thought of as their own?

Cora sped up as the door of the bathroom came into view ahead of her. She pushed it open with a fast, vicious motion, relieved to see that the bathroom was as empty as the rest of the school. The floor was covered in candy-colored tile, and some past student had painted rainbows along the walls, up onto the ceiling, turning the room into a swirl of vibrant, living color. The window was thick carnival glass, red and blue and green and yellow. There were no curtains, because they weren't needed even a little bit: no one trying to look in would be able to see anything aside from color. It was peaceful. It was perfect.

The thought of climbing into the massive bathtub was enough to turn Cora's stomach, but the dryness in her skin and throat told her that she didn't actually have a choice. She needed to spend a certain amount of time soaking every week or risk drying out, which had consequences far more immediate and unpleasant than the minor panic attack that came along with actually taking a bath. She shut and locked the door before peeling off her nightgown and starting the water pouring into the bathtub, taking her time adding three types of sweet-scented bubble bath and two kinds of soaking salt to the bath.

Once the bathtub was full—hot and sweet-smelling and mounded with bubbles, a universe away from the salty, brackish depths that haunted her dreams—she climbed into the water, heart pounding from the conflict between "the water is safe, the water is home and harbor, the water will not hurt you" and "the water is filled with monsters who are only waiting for their opportunity to drag you down." She sank down amid the bubbles until only her face and the blue-green shock of her hair remained uncovered, the rest of her body concealed by the mountain of bubbles that filled the air with rising and falling perfume as they began to pop.

There was always plenty of bubble bath in this particular bathroom, which was also Sumi's favorite, and after her time in Confection, where the ocean was made of strawberry soda and the rivers ran with thick undercurrents of chocolate syrup, Sumi couldn't stand water that smelled or tasted like *water*. Cora had been judgmental before their time in the Moors, and now she was grateful.

She wasn't as fond of the scent of water as she used to be, either.

Slowly, the heat from the bath sank into her bones, warming them, chasing away the shadows of the Drowned Gods, reminding her that she was a mermaid, and for a mermaid to be afraid of drowning was ridiculous. This was where she belonged. This was where she'd come from, and where she would eventually go, when the Trenches saw how sincerely she wanted to come home and swung their watery doors open for her a second and final time. This world wasn't hers to keep. She wasn't staying here.

Cora's eyes fluttered shut as sleep reclaimed her, and in the soup of bubbles and slowly cooling water, she slipped under

the surface, down to where it was warm, and sweet, and welcoming. She was a mermaid, after all.

All she needed was a little more time, and she'd be going home.

2 ECHOES OF THE UNHEARD

CORA KNEW THAT THERE was nothing wrong with her. She'd been hearing it since she was in preschool, and when you hear a thing often enough, you start to understand it, even if you'd rather not. Sometimes she thought she would have been happier if there *had* been something wrong with her, if there *had* been something she could chase after and fix.

But no. There was nothing wrong with her. She was the inevitable result of generation after generation of people struggling to live through starvation, to keep the fat from their rare times of plenty on their bones for long enough to coax a little more living from a land that was all too frequently hostile to their needs. She had been a chubby baby, and a chubby child, and the first time someone had called her "fat" in the tone of voice that made it perfectly clear they were trying to insult her more than they were trying to describe her, she'd been barely five years old.

She'd gone on her first diet when she was eight years old. All the books she'd read since then said children shouldn't be on diets when they were still growing, that all she'd done by trying to fix the shameful reality of her existence was slow her own metabolism and make her fatness even more of a foregone conclusion, but she'd been a little kid. She'd been lonely, since the other kids were getting more and more reluctant to play with her, as if fat was somehow contagious, and she'd been scared—not of her size, which was normal and natural and didn't slow her down in any way, but of the way the world was responding to it. She'd heard one of the student teachers talking to a playground attendant in the low, hushed voice of an adult who assumed she wasn't in earshot, saying that what her parents were doing to her was child abuse.

Cora came from a loving home, but she knew what happened if someone accused your parents of abusing you. She even knew why it had to happen, because Johnny from her kindergarten class used to come to school with bruises shaped like boots in the middle of his back, black and purple and terrifying. But she didn't want to be taken away because someone thought her body was broken and didn't bother to ask her what she ate at home before they made a phone call that set a terrible thing into motion. So she decided to take the problem into her own hands.

Everyone said losing weight was just a matter of eating less and moving more, and so for three weeks she'd skipped breakfast by dragging her feet through the process of getting ready for school, thrown her lunch away, and then spent dinner moving the food around her plate with a fork, rather than putting it into her mouth. And she'd spent recesses and lunch racing around the blacktop like a wild thing, waiting for the fat to fall away and the slim, beautiful girl she dreamed of being to emerge.

Instead, she'd collapsed in the middle of the afternoon on Thursday of the third week, too exhausted and malnourished to move, and the call to child services had been made anyway, by the school nurse, who assumed her parents had been starving her.

Her mother's expression of genuine shock and horror when she arrived at school had probably gone a long way toward keeping Cora's feared consequences from materializing. Instead,

she'd received a thorough checkup, a firm order to eat her dinner from now on, and a referral to a therapist who specialized
in childhood eating disorders.

There was nothing wrong with her diet. She ate healthy
foods, in reasonable amounts, and sweets and candies, in the
same amounts as her peers; she just had a body that wanted
to hold on to things a little tighter, keep them a little closer,
in case of some future famine or struggle. She was active on
the playground and in youth sports when her parents enrolled
her, finding joy first on the soccer field and then on the swim
team, where her size was nothing compared to the strength of
her arms and her ability to propel herself through the water.

There was nothing wrong with any part of her. She was
healthy, and happy, and fat, something which everyone who
met her was quick to point out, some in tones of gleeful disgust, others in tones of shameful condemnation. Did she not
know that she was fat, perhaps? Had she missed that essential
fact of her own physical reality, and needed it explicitly explained to her? There was nothing wrong with her, but she
was smart enough to know that everything was wrong with
her, and even the fact that her parents and her doctors said that
dieting would only do her harm didn't change the fact that
if she didn't find a way to magically become thin, she would
never be accepted.

Even people who were quick to say that certain words
shouldn't be said because they were like throwing rocks at
people over things they couldn't help were happy to laugh
when the fat kid fell down on the blacktop, even if she stood
up bleeding. "You could choose not to be fat," they would
always say, when she called them on it. "If you just had a little
self-control, there'd be nothing to make fun of you for. We're
doing you a favor."

So she'd eaten less and less, even as her doctors and parents tried to get her to eat more, she'd learned to sit so as to take up as little space as possible, and when the laughter and the cruelty had echoed so loudly in her ears that she couldn't hear anything else, she had given herself over to the water, which had only ever cared for her, had only ever welcomed her home.

When she had filled her lungs with water and felt her body start to drift away on a sweet, liquid tide, her last thought had been that she was finally going home, finally going to a place where everyone would be able to see that there was nothing wrong with her. Then everything had gone black, and when she had woken up again, it had been, not in a hospital bed, but in the tangled kelp forest of the Trenches, and everything had changed.

"See, that's how we know you really went through a door, and didn't just have a near-death experience that *felt* like going through a door," Kade had said, when she first came to the school, still unsteady on the legs she no longer thought of as her own, unable to shake the feeling that she was going to suffocate in the endless emptiness of the open air. "The other lifeguards at the beach where you went into the water told everyone your body was swept away by the current."

Cora had seen their Facebook updates about the "tragedy" of seeing their "beloved classmate" drown. Some of them had managed to make digs at her weight and how ridiculous it was to think the currents could work fast enough to disappear her enormous bulk, even as they'd claimed to have been her closest friends and confidants. She was reasonably sure that if she had actually had that many friends, she would never have tried to drown herself.

"The Trenches would have found another way to have you if you'd been happy enough to keep dry," Sumi had said, practically, when Cora had confessed her suicide attempt. "My door tried to get me three times before I finally pushed it open, and it would have kept on trying for as long as I was suited to Confection. They know what we need."

"But how?"

Sumi hadn't had an answer to that one.

Cora had been in the Trenches for a year and a half, diving deeper every day, fighting the Serpent of Frozen Tears with the other mermaids, flirting with sirens and chasing currents for the glory of the queen. Then had come the dreadful day when she was swept into one of the Serpent's whirlpools, and the reaching hands of her sisters hadn't been enough to anchor or to save her, and she'd woken on a beach back in the world of her birth, tail split down the middle into two familiar, unwanted legs, scales gone, fins and gills and freedom gone. All she'd been left with was her hair, which now grew in a deep blue-green, a perfect complement to the fins she no longer had.

She'd staggered up the beach naked and starving and half-delirious, unsure where she was or how she'd gotten there, and the first tourists to see her had called the local police, convinced that she had been attacked. The police, in turn, had called her parents, and they'd come laughing and crying down to the station to collect her, asking her over and over again where she'd been. But she'd already heard the officers snickering at the naked fat girl, and she already knew that telling her parents she'd tried to drown herself and turned into a mermaid instead wasn't going to get her very far, so she'd turned her face away and stammered excuses, claiming not to know, not to remember, not to *understand*.

She'd lasted three months in the wreckage of her old life, suddenly sixteen, suddenly remarkable because she'd disappeared, because her hair stood out in a crowd, because she had somehow learned the trick, during the time she claimed not to remember, of dyeing her eyebrows.

Then one of the other girls on the swim team had broken the silent agreement not to look at the fat girl during post-pool shower time, and the news that Cora cared enough about her "new look" to dye her *pubic hair* had spread around school before the end of the day. She'd gone home mortified and crying, and when the next morning came, she had simply refused to get out of her bed.

The next day, Eleanor West had been on their doorstep, pleasantly dotty in a knee-length rainbow raincoat over a bright peach dress that somehow managed to skirt the color "pink" in all but implication, a smile on her face and a pamphlet about her school for children like Cora in her hands.

Cora's parents had been reluctant to listen to a sales pitch for sending their daughter away from home when she'd only just returned from an adventure she still steadfastly insisted she didn't remember, but Cora had looked at Eleanor and seen something familiar in the older woman's eyes, something that spoke to understanding where she'd been and what she'd been through. At Cora's insistence, her parents had allowed Eleanor to explain what she had to offer, and when offered a fresh start, with no one who remembered who she'd been before she disappeared, Cora had leapt at the chance to go.

She'd believed she was never going to see her family again when she'd given herself over to the Trenches, had mourned them and buried them in the hallowed ground of her heart, where they could rest. Leaving them a second time was a promise kept, not a loss. And for them, she was their miracle girl, returned by the sea, and they knew she didn't dye her hair, and they knew that she was miserable, and they knew that whatever was broken inside her was something they couldn't fix, and so they let her go.

Cora Miller walked away from her childhood home with her head held high and her knees barely shaking, convinced that she had finally found the place where she belonged.

Now, as she stood outside Eleanor's office with her fist raised to knock on the door, unable to quite commit to finishing the gesture, she felt the last of her conviction crumbling away, washed out to sea by the constant erosion of her fear.

The door swung open, still untouched. Cora shrank back.

Eleanor, standing framed by the narrow opening, offered her a wan smile.

"It's all right, dear," she said. "I've been waiting for you. I suppose you had best come inside."

3 FULL FATHOM FIVE

ELEANOR'S OFFICE WAS THE only room in the school designed more for the comfort of people who hadn't been to the other side of an impossible door than those who had. The main foyer boasted a chandelier made of crystals that had once been Eleanor's own tears; the kitchen looked like it had been ripped half from an industrial cafeteria and half from a medieval recreation village. Every other room in the house had been touched by the reality of its residents, but in Eleanor's office, it was possible to pretend that this was just another boarding school, one for students who had survived and started to recover from personal tragedy.

Eleanor herself smiled warmly at Cora as she walked around the bulk of her desk and settled in her leather-backed chair, gesturing for Cora to sit in one of the more modest chairs on the other side of the desk. Cora settled without a word of complaint, her still-damp nightgown sticking to her skin, while her hair sent rivulets of water down her back. The upholstery might get wet, but Eleanor wouldn't care about that. Caring about things getting wet wasn't very nonsensical, and Eleanor's devotion to the Nonsense still waiting for her on the other side of her own door was one of the school's few true constants.

(No one knew the name of Eleanor's world, not even Kade, who would inherit the school on the day when she finally felt her grasp on reality had grown flexible enough to allow her to return to her beloved Nonsense to die. But Eleanor's door was one of the rare stable ones, and everyone *did* know that she could go back whenever she felt the time was right.)

"So," said Eleanor.

"So," echoed Cora, and that was where her courage deserted her. All the words she'd been working her way toward saying dried up on her lips, and she looked down at her hands, folded neatly in her lap, dry and unwebbed and dancing with oilslick rainbows.

The rainbows never left her anymore. She would never have believed that she could hate color as much as she did.

"They still speak to you?" asked Eleanor.

Cora's head snapped up. "Every night," she whispered. "They . . . they want me. They think I belong to them because they held me for a few minutes. They won't leave me alone."

"And you think that it's because your door is still propped open, just that little crack, that sliver held by hope. You think if you could let it close, they'd have to let you go." Eleanor pursed her lips, agony in her eyes. "You're wrong, you know. The doors never completely leave us. Even the ones who lose all desire to resume their journeys, even the ones who forget, they're always more vulnerable—"

But Cora wasn't listening anymore. She had seized on the only part of Eleanor's speech that mattered, leaping to her feet and reaching across the desk for Eleanor's hands. "Yes, forget," she said. "I want to forget. I want to be normal again. I want my hair to be brown and the air to feel natural and to go home and sleep in my own bed and see my parents every morning when I wake up." She stopped there, waiting for Eleanor to reply. Seconds slithered past, the silence unbroken until Cora herself took a deep breath, and said, "You've always said that there was a second school."

Eleanor pulled her hands away. "The Whitethorn Institute. Cora, you can't intend—"

"You said they steal your students sometimes. That when you're not fast enough, or when the children are having a harder time adapting to life in this reality, that sometimes Whitethorn gets there first." She sat up straight, giving Eleanor a challenging look. "You said it was where students go when they want to believe that everything that happened on the other side of the door was just a dream, or a delusion, and not a real thing at all. Please. I want to wash the Moors off my skin. I want to drain the Drowned Gods out of my soul. I can't do either of those things here, where I'm expected to dwell and dwell and dwell on what happened. Please. You have to let me go."

Eleanor was silent for a moment, eyes wide and frightened. Finally, she asked, "Have you discussed this with the others?"

Cora didn't need to ask who Eleanor meant by "the others." They had been viewed as a unit by the rest of the student body since their return from the Moors—a third trip through a door that hadn't been meant for most of them. The first had been to the Halls of the Dead, and the second to Confection, where they'd arranged for Sumi's resurrection. Sumi sulked sometimes, because Confection was *her* door, and so she was only looked at with the awe afforded to someone who had died and come back again, and not with the awe that was directed at her fellow travelers.

But still, they were a unit now, a posse, a gang in the teen-movie sense of the word, friends bonded by common adventure and experience. Cora, Kade, Christopher, and Sumi. And now here, in this office, Cora was alone.

She shook her head. "No," she said miserably. "The Moors don't want any of them, even though they all have hooks the Drowned Gods could use if they wanted to try." Sumi had been dead. Christopher loved the dead. Kade had no door to go back through, even if he'd wanted to; Prism had rejected him completely. He could have given himself over to the Moors, and the Drowned Gods could have taken his loyalties without a fight. But they had chosen Cora. The Moors had chosen Cora.

She understood some things about the Moors, in a half-formed way that was almost impossible for her to articulate. She understood that they were a single organism, a great factory whose purpose was transformation, and they made all they owned over in their own image.

The Moors made monsters. Cora was already a mermaid. She didn't want to wake up one day as something worse.

Cora shuddered. "I haven't discussed this with them. Please. I can't live like this. I need to forget. I need the Drowned Gods to let me go."

The tension in the room was like a sheet of glass, thick but fragile, easily shattered and capable of becoming a weapon when it did. Eleanor took a breath, opening her mouth, and Cora tensed against the hammerblow that was about to land.

Someone knocked at the door.

Eleanor froze. Cora did the same. Then, as if cued, they turned in uneasy unison to look toward the source of the sound. "Yes?" called Eleanor, voice surprisingly steady, as if she hadn't been in the middle of an emotionally charged conversation about Cora's entire future.

The door creaked open and a girl poked around the edge. Her face was too thin, too narrow, and too pointed, seemingly made entirely of angles and bruises waiting for the chance to happen. Her hair was a wild mop of carroty curls, too orange to fit any modern definition of "attractive," too bright to be overlooked in a crowd. Her eyes were equally bright, hazel trending toward yellow; she looked like the consequence of some misguided wizard deciding that the fox kits in his back-yard would be happier as human children, without taking their desires into account in the slightest. She looked roughly Cora's age, somewhere in her late teens, in that timeless, breathless pause between childhood and adulthood, when anything was possible, when anything could happen.

"I lost my roommate again, but I found your missing keys." Antoinette held up something so crusted with mud that it looked more like a clod of dirt than anything as useful as keys. If Cora squinted, however, she could see the curve of a key-ring, the angle of a filthy, rotted rabbit's foot, now half-skeletal from its time spent in the ground.

Eleanor startled in her seat, sitting up straighter, eyes bright-ening. "I lost those twenty years ago," she said. "However did you . . . ?"

"I can find anything," said Antoinette, looking briefly, com-pletely peaceful as she put the keys down on the table nearest the door. "I found your keys, and see, there's my roommate. And I wouldn't have had an excuse to knock and find her if I hadn't already found them, so it all makes sense if you put it in a line."

"We know, dear," said Eleanor. "But Cora and I are in the middle of something important right now, so if you don't mind . . ."

"Oh." Antoinette blinked. "All right. I'll see you in class, Cora." She slipped out of the room, closing the door again behind herself.

Cora returned her attention to Eleanor. The tension in the room was broken now: they were just two people, a teacher and a student, having a long-overdue conversation about that stu-dent's future. Cora knew how to navigate those conversations, had been in them time and time again, when she'd wanted to be a lifeguard and the swim coach had come to argue her case to the park administrator who'd wanted to claim her size would be a liability; when she'd wanted to try out for the spring musical, and the drama teacher had tried to gently imply that she might be better off behind the scenes. Being a fat child meant knowing how to be your own best advocate, and Cora advocated very well indeed.

"Whitethorn is . . ." Eleanor trailed off. "It's different. It's very different. I haven't been there in years, and I view it as a personal failing every time I lose a student to them. I never thought that you would be at risk."

"Miss West, *please.*" Cora shook her head. "I can't go back to the Trenches as I am now. The Drowned Gods have too much of a hold on me, and if they followed me . . ." She shuddered. If they followed her into those warm, sunlit waters, she would be bringing a doom far greater than the Serpent down on the heads of those who had never done anything but show her kindness and welcome her home.

By saving Jack's future, she had sacrificed her own. The rainbows dancing over her skin were proof enough of that.

Eleanor took a sharp breath. "We can't be sure that the Whitethorn Institute would be able to sunder you from the Drowned Gods, even if they were to try," she said. "Divinity is a terrible thing, and we try to avoid offending it when we can."

"We have to do *something.* I can't sleep, I can't eat, even swimming hurts me. Please." Cora looked Eleanor in the eye. "I've already tried to kill myself once. If they keep whispering to me, I'm going to try again, and this time, I'm going to succeed."

Eleanor was silent for a long moment before she said, in

a small voice, "That was a low, mean thing to say, Cora. I thought better of you."

"The truth isn't always kind," said Cora. "Please. You're the only one who can help me. You have to help me. Please."

Eleanor looked at her, and she looked at Eleanor, and neither one of them said anything at all.

After the silence had stretched out too long to stand, Cora rose and walked, still in her damp nightgown, toward the office door. "I know you'll have to talk to my parents before you can have me transferred to another school," she said. "Please make sure they understand that this is what I want. This isn't something that's being forced on me by someone else."

Eleanor was silent as Cora turned to leave the room. Only when the girl was standing in the doorway did she place her hands over her face and say, miserably, "But this *is* something that's being forced on you, my darling. This isn't a choice you would ever have made on your own."

The empty room gave her no answer. Cora was gone. After a long moment of renewed silence, Eleanor lowered her hands before she rose and crossed the room to retrieve the ring of keys Antoinette had carried back to her. The keys gave no answer either, and Eleanor was weeping as she turned back to her desk.

In the hall, Cora walked bathed in sunlight, forcing her chin to stay high when it wanted to sink toward her breastbone, to make her smaller. She always wanted to make herself smaller, to take up less space, to avoid the moment when someone would look at her and say with their eyes that she took up more space than she deserved, than she had earned, than she could possibly pay for. It was a hard impulse to fight, and she had so little energy left for fighting anything, apart from the terrible whispers in the dark. She was shaking and exhausted by the time she reached her room, and ducked gratefully inside.

The room was empty, save for the detritus of two teenage girls forced into a small shared space. Cora made her way to her own dresser, pulling her nightgown off over her head, and went digging for clean clothes.

Once she was dressed, she raked a brush through her hair and moved back toward the door. This was still a school, for all that half its students had no interest in any subjects they could learn here in the world of their birth, and the state had certain requirements around attendance and standardized tests. Their teachers worked as much for the state as for Eleanor, and couldn't be trusted to cover for students who stopped going to class.

Cora's legs felt like they were made of lead, almost too heavy to lift. She hadn't had a decent night's sleep in weeks, and she hadn't had anything to eat, despite having been out of bed for hours. Ploddingly, she made her way out into the hall. There would be time to grab something from the dining hall before she had to go to English class. The thought of trying to analyze the poetry of Emily Dickinson without calories was enough to make her want to cry. Why adults constantly wanted to know what centuries-old poems *meant* was beyond her. Shouldn't someone have found the right answer by now? Or at least an answer good enough to accept?

The dining hall was virtually deserted this late in the morning. Only Kade was there, clearing a table that had probably been occupied by the rest of her friends until the bell rang. He looked up at the sound of her footsteps, initially surprised, then smiling.

"Hey, Cora," he said, Oklahoma drawl softening his words

like honey drizzled over a hard biscuit. "We missed you this morning. You still not sleeping well?"

Cora could hide the reason for her nightmares, but she couldn't hide that they were happening, not with Antoinette sleeping in her room and waking up more often than not to the sound of screaming. Still, she forced a smile and said, "I wanted a bath more than I wanted an early breakfast." A small untruth, not even entirely a lie, and Kade wasn't one of the kids who'd come back from his adventures with the ability to sniff out falsehoods like they were rotting meat. She was grateful for that, especially when he laughed and nodded his acceptance of her statement.

"Mermaids and bathtubs," he said. "I bet they didn't have strawberry bubble bath in the Trenches, huh?"

"I don't like the strawberry stuff too much," she said. "It reminds me of Confection."

Kade nodded again, more solemnly. Their time in Confection hadn't been as traumatic as their time in the Moors, but Christopher had still almost drowned, and that sort of thing wasn't worth dwelling on. "Sorry," he said.

"It's all right." The hot food had already been cleared away, but there were still trays of baked goods and whole fruit. Cora hesitated for only a moment before selecting two pears and a blueberry muffin, all things she could carry with her in a napkin to avoid being late to class. The teachers didn't care if their students ate during class, as long as they weren't being actively disruptive. "We can't make things that happened not have happened by wishing that they hadn't." She paused. "Did that sentence even make sense?"

"Enough," he said. "You've got English up first, yeah?"

"Yeah," said Cora, cheeks flushing softly red under their veil of rainbow. Sometimes she thought Kade might be flirting, with the way he kept track of her schedule and noticed when she missed meals. But he couldn't possibly be flirting, not when everyone said the last girl he'd shown an interest in was Nancy. Tall, willowy, *slender* Nancy. He'd never said anything about Cora's body—or anyone's, really—but he didn't have to. Cora had learned long before the Trenches what kind of girls got flirted with, and what kind didn't.

And one way or another, she was leaving soon anyway.

"I'll walk you to class," he said, and fell in step beside her as she left the dining hall and started toward the wing where the classrooms were kept, most of them no larger than the sleeping rooms, none of them set up in the standard, industrial way of her pre-Trenches schools. No plastic seats, no tidy rows of desks. Everything was a comfortable jumble, designed to keep students as comfortable as possible without actually lulling them to sleep.

They walked in an easy rhythm, Cora nibbling at her muffin, Kade filling the silence with amiable small talk about the embroidery project he was working on, which seemed to involve stitching a dizzying array of songbirds onto the back of a denim jacket. In the blinking of an eye and less than half a blueberry muffin, he was saying he'd see her at lunch, and leaving her standing in front of her English classroom door, blinking after him.

The room was only half full. It was easy enough to get her preferred armchair, deep and plush enough not to dig into her sides, close enough to the back of the room to avoid making her a target if the teacher needed to force someone to participate. She settled, nibbling at her muffin, and only half-listened as class got underway.

The teacher was droning on about the iconography of death

in Dickinson's poems when the door cracked open and Sumi stuck her head inside, beckoning to Cora.

"Eleanor-Elly asked me to come get you," she said.

Cora gathered her things, rose, and went.

4 THE WHITETHORN INSTITUTE

ALL TOLD, TRANSFERRING SCHOOLS was an easier process than Cora would have expected. It helped that Whitethorn was hungry for new students: as long as someone was willing to verify that a student fit their entrance requirements, they were more than happy to have them.

Eleanor had only looked Cora in the eyes once since the process began, her pen hovering over the transfer form. "Your parents have agreed to this," she'd said, the unspoken "against my advice" hovering over every syllable. "But you have to understand that entering Whitethorn is easy. Leaving is far less so. You might not be able to come home if you change your mind."

"I won't change my mind," Cora had replied, trying not to look at the rainbows dancing over her fingers, poisonous and lovely. "Please."

Eleanor had sighed then, the sound like bones rattling down in the dark, and signed the paper.

Three days later, the car came for her. She had told no one she was leaving, not even Antoinette, who thought she was simply being transferred to another room at the school; she stood outside, back and shoulders straight, her worldly possessions in two suitcases at her feet, and she did not look back, and she did not cry. For the first time in her life, she was leaving a place she loved because she had *chosen* to do so, and there was power in that.

The car that would take her to the airport was sleek and black, almost featureless. When she climbed into the back, she found the package containing her new uniform waiting for her. She shied away from it at first, unaccustomed to the idea of wearing clothing selected by someone else, but by the time they pulled up at the terminal, she had the bundle in her lap, ready to change and embark on her new life.

She changed in the airport bathroom. Her ticket, provided by the Whitethorn Institute, placed her in a window seat, and to her immense relief there was no one in the seat next to her. She watched out the window as the land fell away, eyes turned toward the shadow of the wood, and tried to convince herself that she could still see the school, that she wasn't sneaking away like a coward while her friends waited for her, that she wasn't running away.

But of course she was. Her eyes drifted shut an hour or so into the flight, and she woke with a jolt when the wheels touched down, jerking her out of her mercifully dreamless sleep. A man was waiting for her at the baggage claim, holding a sign with her name on it, wearing a jacket whose insignia matched the one now stitched above her right breast. Cora went with him willingly, climbing into another black sedan and leaning back against the seat, ready for her new life to begin.

The first thing she noticed as they drove out of the city and approached the Whitethorn Institute was the wall. Not content to circle the school and its associated grounds, it had been expanded, one careful brick and land acquisition at a time, to enclose a full three miles of forest. The trees loomed dark and foreboding above it, their branches locked together as if they sought to make a second wall, this one to bar the birds, the wind, the very sky itself.

Made of thick gray stone, mottled with moss and lichen,

the Whitethorn Institute's wall gave every impression of having grown up out of the bedrock. It was immoveable, unbroken, ten feet high and utterly featureless. There was no razor wire along the top, no floodlights; they weren't necessary. She could tell just by looking at it that no one had ever successfully escaped from the grounds. She would learn later that the few students who had managed to reach the wall had proven unable to scale it, and even if they had, they would have found themselves in the middle of nowhere, far from any chance of rescue.

The car slid smoothly down the road, paralleling the long gray line of the wall. Cora kept her eyes on the window, tracing every detail of her new landscape. The wall was ominous, but she'd seen worse; it was only a pale echo of the menace contained in the smallest outhouse in the Moors. In the moment, her shoes seemed like a far greater problem than the wall.

They pinched. Everything else was sized perfectly, but the shoes were too tight. It was a simple, monochrome uniform: black shoes, white socks, gray skirt, white shirt with black tie, and over the top of it all, a black jacket with a stylized *W* and *I* ringed with a chevron of thorns stitched above her right breast. The insignia should have seemed silly, even childish. Instead, it seemed like a threat. Try to run, and you would bleed; try to get away, and you would be ensnared.

The gates of the institute swung open. The car turned down the driveway, and the Whitethorn Institute swallowed another incoming student alive.

PART II

THE STUDENT BODY

5 A WORLD WITHOUT RAINBOWS

THE FRONT HALL OF the Whitethorn Institute seemed to have been designed by a team of people dedicated to stamping out all hints of imagination. The walls were polished oak; the floor was gray marble, lined with industrial rugs to keep students from slipping. Cora stepped onto that floor, tight new shoes clicking against the stone, and swallowed, her hair suddenly feeling like some huge and unspeakable offense. It was a color that didn't belong here, had never belonged here, and should have been washed away before she brought it to sully this pristine place.

The conviction that *she* didn't belong here was beginning to coil in her chest, tight and heavy as the Serpent. She swallowed, forcing herself to keep breathing through the first stirrings of panic, and walked on, waiting to hear her driver's footsteps echoing her own.

She heard no such thing. The man who had brought her to the school's gates, helped her bring her suitcases to the door, was not following. He had retreated back to his car as soon as his duty was done, leaving her to move onward alone. This was her school now. This was her home. She might not belong here yet, but she would. She had to.

She'd signed all of her choices away.

The hall was straight and easy to follow, leading inexorably toward a single conclusion. Cora took a deep breath and kept walking, summoning the courage that had seen her go from drowned girl to mermaid to Drowned Girl, capital letters and all. She had been swept into the Trenches because she needed them, and she had become a hero there because heroism had always been in her, a hard core of sharpened coral as strong as steel tempered in her soul. It was that core she gathered around her now, and used to keep herself moving forward.

The only thing that made her courage shiver and try to shrink away was the cold that filled the hall, gray and unforgiving, inimical to the silver glitter of the depths. There was no glitter here, and every breath was another kind of drowning. Cora shivered, tightening her fingers on the handles of her suitcases, and kept walking. If she stopped moving here, she would never start again.

And she had come of her own free will. If anyone was at fault here, it was her. No one was coming to save her.

This was how she saved herself.

The hallway ended at a tall mahogany door, unmarked, like the person on the other side knew without a doubt that anyone who made it this far would know who they were. Cora stopped, blinking silently, and waited for something to happen. The echoes of her footsteps faded, until all that remained in the hall was an absolute, swallowing silence. The door swung open. The man on the other side regarded her with quiet sympathy, eyes going first to her hair, and then to her waistline, and finally to her face—a progression she knew all too well. Cora bristled, but said nothing.

He was tall, not only in relation to Cora herself, but in relation to the world around him; he made the man who had picked her up at the airport look like he'd been built to a slightly different, considerably more reasonable scale. He was neither old, like Miss Eleanor, nor young, like Cora, but somewhere in the measureless, interminable middle, where he could have laid claim to almost any age and been believed. A scar ran from the right side of his jaw and down the length of his neck, vanishing into the starched collar of his white button-down shirt. It was the only truly eye-catching thing about him. Terrifying as he was—more through the weight of his presence than through any single aspect of his being—Cora felt as though she could forget him in an instant, as though taking her eyes off of him for a second would be to risk losing track of him forever. There was nothing about him to hang a memory on.

Nothing except for that scar.

"Thank you for coming here so promptly," he said, eyes remaining settled on her face. It was like being pinned under glass, held somehow captive. The sudden urge to run seized her, almost uncontrollably strong. She was here because she wanted to be, and she still wanted to run. Even if she didn't make it to freedom, she'd know she'd tried. She'd have that much to hold on to.

"Miss Miller," said the unremarkable man.

Cora froze.

"It's an admirable thought," he continued. "Most of our students think to run, but relatively few think to try it during intake. I'm impressed. Attention on me, please."

Cora swallowed hard and fixed her eyes on the unremarkable man's face.

He smiled. It was a pleasant, paternal expression that did nothing to render him more memorable. "I am Headmaster Whitethorn; welcome to the Whitethorn Institute. I've read your file. I'm thrilled you're going to be joining us. I think you'll be an excellent addition to the Whitethorn family, and I believe we can help you. The first step is always admitting you need help, and you've already taken that step by requesting a transfer into our company."

Cora let go of her suitcases and started, for some inane reason, to curtsey. She caught herself before she could complete the gesture, freezing with her hands on the skirt of her uniform, feeling utterly foolish.

"I made a mistake," she said, and her lips were numb, and her tongue was too big for her mouth. But this place, this place was so big and so cold, and this was just a different way to drown. The Drowned Gods would still be able to find her here. If traveling to a different *world* hadn't been enough to break their hold on her, why would she think that a few miles would make any difference at all? All her bravery had been spent on making it this far; she had no more left to spare. Voice small and pockets empty, she managed to continue, "I'm sorry to have wasted your time. I want to go home."

"Miss West is a trifle eccentric, and her teaching standards fail to align with our own, but she has never struck me as incompetent," said the headmaster. He fixed her with a steely eye. "Are you saying that she sent you here without signing the transfer papers?"

"N-no," stammered Cora. "I signed everything, but—"

"And your parents, Miss Miller. I believe they signed the papers as well? And those papers included detailed information regarding this school's legal obligation to our students?"

"Yes," said Cora, voice still small.

"Then I'm sure you understand that this *is* your home now, and this *is* where you belong, by your own choice and admission. You signed the paperwork. You are allowed one call off-campus a week, on Friday afternoon; if you wish to call your parents then and begin the process of removing yourself from our custody, that is your right." His lips drew back in what someone less afraid might have called a smile. Cora flinched. There was something disturbing about the expression, almost disturbing enough to make him memorable. Not quite, though. She knew that if she looked away, or even blinked too long, she'd forget everything about him.

"You know all about running away, don't you, Miss Miller?" he asked. His voice was soft and lilting as he continued: "There was a door. Your file doesn't go into detail as to its nature— psychiatrists always forget the most essential parts of the story, I find—but there was a door where a door wasn't meant to be, in a wall or in the pattern rain makes on the sidewalk, etched in chalk or scrawled in shadow. There was a door, and it called to you somehow. It *knew* you. It wanted to be opened, and you, poor child, poor, innocent child, you were naïve enough to open it."

Cora felt as if her blood had been replaced by seawater, cold and thin and sluggish in her veins. She couldn't move. She could barely breathe.

"I know it will take time for you to trust me enough to tell me what you found on the other side of the door. I know it was a world where the rules were different, or where it seemed like there were no rules at all. A world where you could live your most ridiculous, decadent dreams. I think all children dream of finding a place like that, a place without bedtimes, or lessons, or rules. But children crave structure as much as they crave freedom. They start to dream of it if they go without for too long, and then those beguiling, alluring worlds, those whimsical fantasies, they turn cruel. Yours did, didn't it? It cast you out."

He leaned closer. The smile was gone. For the first time, he was memorable. He was memorable, and he was terrible, and Cora, who had been a hero, who had saved the Trenches, bit the inside of her cheek to keep from crying out in fear.

"It told you to be sure, and it changed you—your hair, your skin, everything you thought immutable about your self—and yet somehow you still weren't sure, and now you're here. You're finally safe, Miss Miller. Everything you experienced happened in another world, in another life, to someone you aren't going to be anymore. We're going to help you."

"How?" whispered Cora.

"We're going to teach you how to forget," said the headmaster, and nothing had ever been so terrible, and nothing had ever been so wonderful.

"I didn't . . . I didn't go through only one door," said Cora. A tear ran down her cheek, so hot it was scalding. "I followed a girl with lightning where her heart was supposed to be through another door, and while I was there, I caught the attention of some . . . some things I shouldn't have. They want to take me and make me their own. I asked to come here because you could help break me free of them. Can you really make them let me go?"

The headmaster smiled again, settling his hand on her shoulder. "Most of the work will be yours, but yes," he said. "We can reconnect you to *this* world, where you belonged all along. We can set you free. All you have to do is make an effort. We only want what's best for our little community. We only want everyone to be well."

"That's all I want," said Cora. She was crying again, with relief, not fear. "I just want to be well."

"That's all anyone wants, in the end," he said. "It doesn't matter why you want it. Here, we don't require you to be sure. Here, we're sure enough for everyone."

He led Cora deeper into the institute, and everything was silent, and everything was still, and the whispers of the Drowned Gods still echoed in the corners of her mind like warnings that she wouldn't get away that easily.

6 JACK-O'-LANTERN GIRLS

THE ALARM WENT OFF promptly at 5:25 A.M., the same way it did every day but Sunday. Cora, who had been awake since shortly after midnight, groaned and pulled her pillow over her face. The Drowned Gods had been getting quieter since she'd entered an environment that refused to acknowledge their existence, but they were getting more desperate at the same time; over the course of the past two months, the whispers had grown more venomous, and twice as barbed as they'd been when she was at Eleanor's. Sleep was still a lie she told herself every night when she closed her eyes, and like all lies, it always let her down.

It didn't help that she had no friends here to offer an alternative to their poisons. A rough hand seized the pillow and jerked it out of Cora's grasp, flinging it across the room. Any sound it made when it hit the wall was covered by the ongoing alarm. Cora sat up, hair in her eyes, and glared, her hands clenching on the blanket, not quite forming fists, but close enough.

"Oh, no," said the girl who stood next to her bed, arms crossed and eyes narrowed. She was tiny, the smallest girl in their dorm, barely four-foot-eleven, with bones like a bird. Cora towered over her when they stood side by side. In the moment, they were almost eye-to-eye. "Punch me if you want, but I'm not letting us get any more demerits because you're too selfish to stop hiding your body glitter and too lazy to get up when the alarm goes off. Out of bed, now. We haven't been inspected in a week. It's our turn."

Cora immediately turned her eyes away, shrinking in on herself, doing her best to vanish behind the curtain of her hair. "M'sorry," she mumbled. "I didn't sleep well last night."

"You never sleep well," said the girl, almost sneering.

Cora couldn't think of a counter for the absolute truth, and so she stood. The rough cotton nightgown she'd been issued along with the rest of her official Whitethorn Institute paraphernalia swirled around her knees, and her skin crawled at the touch of it, like her body was trying to escape from itself. That was nothing new. Her body always felt like it was trying to escape from itself, except when she was in the water. In the water, she felt finished, perfect, *whole.*

The Whitethorn Institute had a swimming pool. She wasn't allowed to use it, wasn't allowed to sign up for any physical education classes that would take her close enough to smell the chlorine, but she still caught whiffs of it on the other girls' skins, and she yearned for its embrace as she had wanted very little else in her life. She wanted to swim. She *needed* to swim. Everything would start making sense if she could just go swimming . . .

But according to the headmaster, if she went swimming, if she even had a *bath,* instead of endless showers, all the ground they'd gained against the Drowned Gods in the last two months would be erased, and she'd be back where she'd started. The rainbows that had been fading from her skin day by day, accusations of hoarded body glitter aside, would come surging back, and she would be lost. The precipice she balanced above was deep, and she needed to be careful.

The dainty girl in front of her sniffed. "Make your bed, and hurry. The alarm's almost over."

As if on cue, the blaring sound stopped, and the pleasant, TV-ready voice of their headmaster came through the intercom.

"Welcome to another beautiful day at the Whitethorn Institute. I trust you're all awake and ready to put all your energy into learning, growing, and becoming better citizens of the world in which we live. It's the only one we have, so we have to take care of it."

The other girls in Cora's room kept straightening their pillows and pulling on their uniforms, not acknowledging the words pouring from the loudspeaker. Cora had been there for two months—far less time than the rest of them—and even she could have recited most of the headmaster's speech from memory. It rarely changed. When it did, the changes were never good. In this place, change never was. "Stability lends serenity" was one of the school's mottos. They were all expected to live by it, and if they didn't want to, there was always someone close at hand to change their minds.

"Get dressed," hissed one of the other girls, slanting a quick, almost panicked look at Cora. "We can't afford any more demerits. We're already at the bottom of the chore list for the next semester."

"And whose fault is *that*?" sneered the dainty girl, tucking the last corner of her blanket under, so that it formed a military-crisp seal, like the whole thing had just rolled off the showroom floor. She cast a quick, venomous look at Cora, who was struggling to get her nightgown over her head with one hand, the other already fumbling for the pieces of her uniform. Her cheeks flared red with the stress of standing naked before the others, but she'd learned the hard way that she didn't have a choice. "We were doing fine until she came along."

"We were not," said the first girl. Her voice took on a strident tone. "We were always on the bottom of the middle. One person isn't enough to drag us down. We rise and fall as a team."

"Keep telling yourself that, Emily," said the dainty girl, and stepped away from her bed, falling into position at the foot with almost military precision.

Cora fastened her bra and yanked her uniform top on over her head and looked quickly around the room, fingers moving on autopilot to do up her buttons. She still had to tie her tie before she'd be considered anything less than naked, but at least this was a start. It was more than she'd had a moment before.

"*Hurry,*" hissed another girl.

Cora set herself to dressing even faster, afraid, as she was every morning, that she would rip something or lose a button in her hurry. She hated the fact that they were expected to dress immediately upon getting out of bed, when their turn at the showers wasn't until after breakfast; it was unhygienic, and even though the rule applied to all of them equally, the consequences of walking around the school smelling of sweat and sleep weren't applied equally to all members of the student body. Cora had learned that the hard way in her pre-Trenches middle school. If a thin, pretty girl smelled bad, it was because she smelled bad that day. If Cora smelled bad, the other girls would say it was because she was fat, would say all fat people smelled bad, all the time. Reminding them about the shower rules wouldn't erase the sneers from their faces.

But her discomfort wasn't going to change anything, not here, not in this place where the needs of the student body as a whole were put ahead of the needs of any individual. And as the daily routine dulled the rainbows on her skin more and more, and quieted the whispers of the Drowned Gods in her ears, she found it easier and easier to forgive and dismiss the parts that rubbed her wrong.

The headmaster was still talking, although he seemed to be winding down. He had already made his usual points about academics—important—and athletics—also important, even though the nature of the school meant they couldn't compete against anyone else, and needed, instead, to compete against each other, dorm fighting dorm, like school was some sort of gladiatorial competition most of them would never stand a chance of winning; all that remained was today's inspirational message, whatever that was going to be.

"We here at the Whitethorn Institute understand that you are going through a difficult period in your lives. Childhood is confusing. Adulthood is even more so. We know that you're fighting against an endless cascade of contradictions. That's why we provide you with a structured environment tailored to help you remember what it means to be a citizen of the world. *This* world, the only one that should ever matter to you. You are home. It may not feel like it right now, but I promise you, one day, you'll remember all the parts of your life that made it so fulfilling before you were led astray."

The girls in the dorm stood perfectly straight and perfectly still at the foots of their beds, arms at their sides, chins lifted, staring at the wall like it was going to reveal all the secrets of the universe.

"I am overjoyed to be able to tell you all that one of our own is going to be graduating today. Regan Lewis has finally put the past behind her, and will be returning to her family, where she will be able to rejoin society. Regan, did you want to say something to the student body?"

"I absolutely do, Headmaster Whitethorn." The new voice was sweet, happy, bland. If oatmeal were a person, it would sound like that girl. Cora resisted the urge to close her eyes.

Once, Regan Lewis had been as bright and alive as anyone.

She had been bright and alive enough to break the rules, to be branded a bad girl and a transgressor and a flight risk, bright and alive enough to find herself walled up in the living tomb of the Whitethorn Institute, where she could never have done anything but die.

"Hello, everyone. My name is Regan Lewis, and I'm going to graduate today. I'm going home to my family and my parents, and I'm going to finish high school with the rest of my class. I'm going to stand next to kids I've known since kindergarten, and it's going to be hard, because they're still going to think of me as the weird girl who spent all her time daydreaming about unicorns, and not the mature citizen that I've become. I'll have to work. The work doesn't end just because I leave. I'll have to—"

She stopped, seeming to struggle with her next words, like they had become stones, like they were sticking in her throat.

"Regan? Are you all right?" The headmaster's voice was gentle, even compassionate. He did care about them, in his way. It was just that his care didn't help them the way he liked to pretend it did. A jack-o'-lantern might be beautiful, but it was still something that had been cut open and hollowed out because someone wanted it to suit their idea of what a pumpkin ought to be. It wasn't its own self anymore.

Cora couldn't wait to be a jack-o'-lantern. Anything that meant she was still *Cora* in some way, and not the puppet of the Drowned Gods. She listened to Regan and she yearned, wishing with everything she had to be in the other girl's shoes.

Regan laughed. The sound was loud and wild and free, was bright and alive, and every head in the room snapped up and swiveled toward the loudspeaker. Emily clapped her hands over her mouth. The dainty girl, whose name Cora still didn't know after sharing a room with her for months—Cora wondered

if the school had taken it away somehow, as a punishment—
looked like she was about to cry. The other two girls, Rowena
and Stephanie, looked as if they'd seen a ghost.

"I can't do it. I'm sorry, and I never wanted to be a hero, but
that doesn't mean I'll let you turn me into a villain." Regan
was suddenly shouting, voice rendered huge and booming by
the intercom. "I won't lie to everyone I care about just because
you want my story to have a different shape, and I won't pretend to be something I'm not. I wish I could, but I can't. I *did*
see unicorns, and I *did* change the world, even if they never
needed me to save it, and I'm going to find my door, and I'm
going to go home, I am, they can't stop me, they can tie me up
and try to break me, but I know a bridle when I see one, and
they can't—"

The intercom cut out in the middle of her sentence. A single tear rolled down the dainty, nameless girl's cheek. Not a
single one of them said a word.

It didn't feel like there was anything for them to say, and
it was almost time for inspection, after all: better not to make
trouble, not now. Not when there were demerits on the line.

Cora stood as still as the rest of them, and wondered how
much longer she had before she would start forgetting.

7 CANDY-COATED NIGHTMARE

DAYS AT THE WHITETHORN Institute always followed the same pattern, as perfect and predictable as a spider's web.

First, the morning alarm, followed by inspection of the dorms, to make sure the girls were out of bed, dressed, and ready to begin their day. Cora wasn't sure what happened in the boys' dorm: the student body was mostly female, and the three male students kept almost entirely to themselves, insular and suspicious and unwilling to talk to anyone they saw as an outsider. She guessed things must be pretty bad for them. There were so few of them, after all.

Or maybe that made things better. When the school wasn't policing the students, the students policed each other. Fewer people in the dorm meant fewer spies and fewer enforcers. The boys might have a level of freedom she didn't. A level of freedom she'd never have again, a level of freedom she had voluntarily surrendered, in exchange for the return of her own future.

After the alarm, they all filed into the cafeteria for breakfast, which was perfectly nutritionally balanced, and assigned according to each student's individual needs. All the meals at Whitethorn were prepared the same way, perfectly tailored, unexchangeable. Cora ate her unsalted eggs, applesauce, and turkey bacon without complaint. She wasn't losing any weight on this industrial diet, but at least the other students couldn't blame that on her. Some of them looked legitimately baffled by the fact that her size hadn't changed, having assumed—often aloud, where she could hear them—that people her size were as big as they were because they lived on nothing but cupcakes and candy, not because their metabolisms were geared for size.

Some of those same students still said terrible things in her hearing, as if their own breakfasts of waffles dripping with honey and butter and whipped cream and even sprinkles were somehow healthy because they belonged to skinny people. Cora hadn't thought about how much she'd miss the brief respite she'd had at Eleanor West's school, where the students had all, by some unspoken consent, restricted their teasing and name-calling to things they'd done or places they'd gone, never targeting people for who they were.

She reminded herself over and over that it was worth it, it had to be worth it, it had to be worth enduring the whispers of her classmates if it meant muffling the whispers of her nightmares.

On Cora's third day, one of the waffle-eaters had tried to trade trays with her, and looked baffled when Cora had responded by pulling her oatmeal defensively closer to herself.

"Take it, silly," the girl had said. "We both know you're dying for the sugar. So take mine, and give me yours, and we can both live happily for another fifteen minutes." Clearly the girl expected her offer to be accepted. She had still been holding out her tray when the heavy hand of one of the school matrons had fallen on her shoulder. Another had fallen onto Cora's, and both of them had been whisked away for a stint in solitary. Cora's skin still crawled when she looked at that particular girl.

The girl didn't look at Cora at all.

After breakfast came classes, all of them moving from room to room, learning facts and figures from one set of teachers, learning the way the world worked, learning the way to think and act and be.

It had been a shock for Cora, on her first day, when she'd walked into one of those classes and seen a poster hanging in front of the whiteboard, labeled THE COMPASS in large, stark letters. They named the dimensions differently, called Nonsense and Logic "Delusion" and "Compulsion," called Wickedness and Virtue "Recklessness" and "Austerity," but the pattern was the same. All the old familiar branches and divides, twisting out into infinity, like the branches of a tree. Somewhere in that pattern were the Trenches; somewhere in that pattern was her home, her promised place, where she would be able to sleep easy for the rest of her life.

But the Moors were there too. The Moors, and the reason she could never go home.

She hadn't realized she was crying until the teacher had walked over and pressed a handkerchief into her hand. Real cotton, the edges expertly hemmed: no noses would be wiped on sleeves here, no twists of tissue tossed aside.

"It's all right, Cora," she had said, and her voice had been warm and kind, and her eyes had been so cold. "I know it's a shock, but we're here to help you through this. We're here to make you well again."

Cora had smiled hesitantly up at her, and hoped she was telling the truth.

After class came sport, which mostly meant running laps around the track, unless you'd been tapped for one of the various athletic clubs, and then it meant playing some game with complicated, tedious rules that never changed. Cora had managed to avoid the athletic clubs so far, largely by dint of not being allowed to swim, and no one believing she could be good at anything else. She was sure the headmaster would eventually order them to invite her, but for now, she was allowed to just run and run and run, sinking into the feel of her feet hitting the ground and the air in her lungs, and all the other aspects of land-life that kept her tethered far from the grasp of the Drowned Gods.

She had always loved to run. She had always been *good* at running. She was still good at running, even if there was nowhere left for her to run to.

On the day when Regan Lewis laughed over the intercom and everything changed, the schedule was still in effect. The sound of Regan's laughter had barely faded before the door opened and one of the matrons stepped inside. Cora stiffened, trying not to show her fear.

The staff of the school—and how strange it was, to be at a school with an actual staff, instead of Eleanor and a few teachers who came during the day and left at night, preferring not to know too much about what went on at the mysterious boarding school full of artists and overdramatic weirdoes! How strange, and how honestly unpleasant—consisted almost entirely of alumni. They had all been through doors of their own, once upon a time. They had traveled to magical lands, places where the sky talked and the sea sang, and they had decided they liked this world better. More, they had decided that because *they* liked this world better, and because their parents had been sad when they were gone, that all the doors should be sealed and locked forever, to keep any more children from going missing.

This wasn't the first time Cora had met people who thought their ideas about how the world should be were the only right ones. It was the first time she'd met them when they were in a position of clear, unquestioned power over her.

This matron, a stiff-faced woman who always wore the

drabbest browns and grays she could find, like she was trying to vanish into the background, was one of the less forgiving. She looked around the dorm, nose wrinkling slightly when she saw Cora's covers, which were still disheveled despite Cora's best efforts to smooth them out. Aloud, she said, "I see an improvement, Cora. You're beginning to take more pride in your things."

"Thank you, matron," said Cora automatically. Failure to thank a matron for praising you could result in demerits, and too many demerits would mean another trip to solitary, another spell spent sitting alone in a room with no windows and no distractions, to think about what she'd done.

Cora didn't *want* to think about what she'd done. Sitting alone in silence just created more openings for the Drowned Gods to slither through, and they didn't need the help.

The matron moved on, shifting her attention to Emily, who stood perfectly straight, perfectly mannered, her eyes fixed ahead of her and a pleasant, almost vapid expression on her face. If Cora hadn't known what all the members of her dorm had in common, she would have thought Emily didn't belong here at all.

Each of the dorms was different. The students who'd gone to Logical worlds got waffles for breakfast and bedtimes that changed every night. They got socks that didn't match and class schedules that shuffled around them like a deck of cards, trying to get them used to the idea that they were back to living in a world where things wouldn't always, couldn't always make sense. The students who'd gone to Nonsense worlds got stricter schedules and regimes than even the Wicked students, rules piled upon rules upon rules until the weight of it crushed the rebellion out of their hearts.

Once they were broken—once the Nonsense kids started

following rules and the Logical kids started disregarding them—they could be moved to new dorms, to start unlearning other habits of behavior. To start allowing themselves to be ground down, disappearing back into the children they had been before they'd needed something different so completely that they'd summoned impossible doors to whisk them away to a place where they could be happy. Where they could be whole.

Emily shivered. The matron stopped in front of her, suddenly as attentive as a wolf scenting a deer in the still of the forest.

"Emily," she said. "Where does your family live?"

"Dublin, Ohio, matron."

"How many siblings do you have?"

"Two. One older, one younger."

"Can scarecrows talk?"

Emily trembled.

The matron narrowed her eyes. "Can scarecrows talk?" she repeated, tone clearly implying that there was only one right answer, and it wasn't the one she expected from Emily.

It hurt, to deny the things the heart knew were true. It *hurt,* and while Emily and Cora weren't friends, Cora understood that the matron was holding out a razor and asking Emily to run it willy-nilly across her body, hoping not to hit an artery.

Silence and blending into the background were Cora's forte. She was *good* at it. But she was also a hero, and heroes didn't stand idly by while someone smaller was victimized.

"Scarecrows don't *talk,*" she scoffed, loudly enough and clearly enough to guarantee she would be overheard. The matron stiffened. Cora acted like she hadn't noticed, continuing blithely, "They're just straw stuffed into old potato sacks. If scarecrows could talk, that would mean straw could talk, and if straw could talk, grass would be able to talk, and no one could mow their lawns."

"Cora," said the matron, through gritted teeth, "I don't believe I was talking to you."

"Oh. I'm sorry, matron." Cora blinked at her, trying to look innocent and confused. "I thought it was a question for anyone. It won't happen again."

"See that it doesn't," said the matron, and moved on to the girl without a name. "You'll be measured this afternoon," and she said a word, her lips moved in a word, but all that came out was the sound of total, perfect silence. "I'm hoping we'll see some growth, aren't you?"

"Yes, matron," said the dainty girl, voice small and tight with fear.

"If we don't, we may have to take more extreme measures." The matron looked around the room, seeming to weigh and measure every inch of it with her eyes. Finally, she sniffed and said, "There will be an assembly this afternoon, to discuss the unfortunate outburst during morning announcements. If any of you are feeling shaky or uncentered, you can request a counseling session after lunch. There's no shame in seeking help, children. Seeking help is the most human thing a person can do."

"Yes, matron," chorused the girls, in unison—even Cora, who felt pride and shame warring in the center of her chest as she spoke, burning her with their fierceness.

"Breakfast will proceed as normal," said the matron, and left the room.

All five girls stood perfectly still and stayed perfectly silent for a count of ten. Sometimes the matrons would close the door, take a breath, and then come back in to catch the girls doing something they weren't supposed to. Seconds ticked by, and the matron did not reappear.

Emily burst into tears.

She cried noisily, messily, with the glorious abandon of a small child racing headlong toward something they weren't supposed to touch. It was the most untidy thing Cora had seen her do so far, and for a moment she stopped and stared at her, even as Rowena and Stephanie rushed to try and calm her down. It didn't work: Emily kept crying, eyes screwed up so tight that they seemed almost like they'd been painted on, black slashes against the dark chestnut brown of her skin.

"Make her stop," snapped the dainty girl, emerging from her own fugue of shock and dismay.

Cora turned slowly to look at the dainty girl without a name, eyes narrowing. She was doing her best to follow the rules and fit in here. The school was cold and gray and sometimes terrifying, but she had come of her own accord, and that made anything she suffered here her own fault. It was a door she should perhaps have left closed, and would have, if not for the Drowned Gods dripping poison in her dreams. If opening *this* door let her close *that* door, then she was happy to have it open. She didn't need to be a mermaid anymore. She didn't need to be a hero.

But that didn't mean she could abide a bully.

Cora stepped in front of the dainty girl, keeping her from reaching Emily. "If she needs to cry, she'll cry," she said. "Leave her alone."

"I'll tell the matrons," said the girl, voice shrill and mean. Cora shrugged and started to turn away. The girl spat, "Whale."

Cora stiffened and turned back. "What did you call me?"

"Whale," repeated the girl, eyes on Cora's own. "Fatty. Stupid pig. Emily's not your friend. No one is. You're too disgusting to have friends."

Cora took a breath, preparing her rebuttal, tears threatening to overwhelm her. The dainty, nameless girl was right: Cora had no friends here. Her friends at Eleanor's school had been incidental, accidents of place and time, and they were far away, and she was never going to see them again. She'd given them up for the chance of freedom. She was as worthless as this girl wanted her to be.

Before she could speak, the door opened again, and the matron reappeared. This was off schedule, and strange; all five of them turned.

Standing next to the matron in the doorway was a short, plumpish girl of Japanese descent, her long black hair tamed into a braid that fell down her back in a single inkslash line. She was wearing a Whitethorn uniform, hands folded demurely in front of herself and eyes cast toward the floor.

"This is Sumiko," said the matron. "She will be taking your open bed. I trust you will all welcome her into our company."

"Hello," said the girl, raising her head and smiling a small, sharp-edged smile. "It's a pleasure to meet you all."

Cora, who had never been expecting to see Sumi again, could only stare in frozen silence as the matron pushed her and her suitcase into the room, then turned and closed the door, leaving the six girls alone.

8 OATMEAL AND OPPOSITION

AS SOON AS THE matron was gone, the other girls swarmed—the dainty, nameless one at the front of the pack. She raked her eyes up and down Sumi's uniformed body, then sniffed.

"I don't see why *we* should get saddled with another new fish," she said. "We're still not finished educating the old one."

"Don't be mean," said Emily.

"Why shouldn't she?" asked Sumi, with what sounded like genuine confusion. "I can tell by the sound of her voice that she's good at it."

The others turned to stare at her. Cora sighed.

"Sumi, why are you here?"

"Antsy can find anything," said Sumi. "She told you so, remember? Well, you went away, and so she knew what she needed to find was you. And when she did, we all talked it over and decided I should be the one to come and get you, since I'm the only one who knows I get to go home when all this is over."

"But you went to Virtue, not Wickedness," said Cora.

Sumi waved a hand, whisking her objections away. "I told them I went to Prism, and Kade's told me enough about that shitbox of a bad cocktail party that I was able to make my case. I'm a Wicked girl now, my admission papers say so."

"Wait, you know each other?" asked Emily. "How do you know each other?"

"We went to school together until the mermaid got scared

and ran away from the whispers in the dark," said Sumi, sympathy in her tone.

The nameless girl stepped forward, expression suddenly furious. "You can't be here and tell lies! Rules are for everyone!" She raised her hand like she was going to slap someone, and hesitated when she couldn't decide quite who.

Sumi didn't so much move as suddenly *had* moved, flowing seamlessly from her position near the door to one directly in front of the other girl, her fingers wrapped tight around her wrist. "Why do you get to decide that?" she asked, tone remarkably reasonable. "What's your name?"

"I'm," said the girl, and her mouth moved, and nothing came out, not a sound, not a whisper, not a hiss. Just a sudden, profound silence, like something had been sliced neatly from the world and tucked aside, where it wouldn't bother anyone. She struggled against Sumi's grip. "Let me *go*."

"I don't want to," said Sumi. "None of this matters. You know that, right? I fought a woman who wanted to have my bones hollowed out so she could store spices inside them, who wanted to make a whole world over in her image, and that mattered more than this, because things made the right kind of nonsense there. I buried my past under a tree with cookies for leaves, and my friends buried me in a garden of bones, and both times I got back up and kept on going, but it wasn't as hard as it is here. I only just got here, but I can already tell this place is . . . it's small. It's hard and it's small and it's *mean*. It knows what's true for you isn't always true for me, and it doesn't care, because it wants to make us all have the same kind of truth and believe in it the same kind of way. It's a bad place. It thinks it's helping and it isn't. So I guess what I wonder is why you're trying to make it even smaller than it already is. They don't like you either. You're not standing outside the cage looking in; you're right in here with us. Why are you like this?"

"Because I'm *not* like you," snarled the dainty girl, twisting free of Sumi's grasp. "Let me guess. You went to a magical world of rainbows and pixies and talking horses, and you had adventures and you saved a kingdom, or maybe a whole bunch of kingdoms, and everybody loved you, because you were a hero. You were made to be loved. You were *perfect*. And then you fell through another door and wound up back with your family, the people who actually cared about you, who didn't just think of you as a magical arm to swing a prophesized sword around, and you didn't know how to love them anymore. You didn't know how to be a *person* anymore. That's why they sent you here. So you could remember how to be a person."

"Is that why your family sent you here?" asked Sumi.

"Sent me?" asked the dainty girl, disbelievingly. "No one *sent* me. This old lady dressed like a circus clown tried to talk me into going to her school, and I would have had to be stupid not to realize she was talking about a place where everyone was going to wallow, forever, in how sad it was that their doors went and closed, even though that was the best thing that could have happened to them. I told her no, and Headmaster Whitethorn showed up the next day. He said I could come here and forget. He said I could be free. So yeah, this place is mean, but it's mean because it has to be. If someone doesn't want to wake up, you have to shake them."

She stuck her nose in the air, like she thought it would somehow make her taller, and stalked out of the room. After a moment's apologetic pause, Rowena followed her. The sound of the door closing behind them was very loud.

Sumi shook her head, looking after them. "That's a girl with a whole lot of angry where her heart's supposed to be." Then she turned back to Cora. "I'm very mad at you, you know. But you need hugs more than you need yelling at, so: hugs?"

Arguing with Sumi was like trying to fight the wind: frustrating, endless, and ultimately pointless. Cora wrapped the smaller girl into a hug, and asked, "Are you the only one here?"

"Of course, silly," said Sumi. "Confection wants me to come home, so this is almost safe for me, or safe as anything gets. Everyone else is back at school, waiting for me to bring you safely back."

"I'm not coming back," said Cora.

Sumi pulled back and stepped away, looking at her with wounded confusion. "But we miss you! You have to come back."

"The Drowned Gods still whisper to me in the night," said Cora. "I have to stay here if I want to be free of them. I can't come back to school."

There was a small cough from the side. Sumi and Cora both turned. Emily was standing there, a faint, almost hopeful smile on her still only half-familiar face, like she thought she might see someone she recognized, like she wasn't entirely sure.

"Do you really think your door's still there?" she asked.

"I know it is," said Sumi. "I've met my daughter, and she hasn't been born yet, and that means Nonsense is going to take me home when it's ready for me."

"The matrons . . ." Emily grimaced. "They want us to say things we know were weren't, and things we know weren't were. They say it's how we break our dependence on delusion. I asked once how it could be a delusion when every one of them knows it really happened, when we were recruited to attend here because of where we went, and they said . . . they said . . ."

She stopped, throat moving soundlessly. Stephanie stepped up next to her, sighed, and said, "They said it didn't matter what we thought the truth was; when the truth isn't something you can see, it's malleable, and because we're still legally children, our parents get to decide what's true for us. They get to say they want their 'real' kids back, the ones they wanted, and not the ones they ended up with."

"Minnie and Cora aren't the only ones who chose to come here—and you, I guess, Sumiko—but there aren't many of them," said Emily, getting herself back under control.

"Minnie?" Sumi cocked her head.

"That's not really her name," said Stephanie. "We don't know much about the world she went to, but we know it had to do with rats, and something about being there stole her real name, so she can say it, but no one hears it. If you knew it, and you said it with her in the room, no one would hear you, either."

That was a terrifying, fascinating thought. "There's not a lot of magic that can make it through the doors and keep hurting you once you're here," said Sumi, glancing to Cora. "Not having a name sounds like it would be really difficult. How could anyone tell you when your pizza was ready?"

"That's why we call her 'Minnie,' but only when she's not in the room," said Stephanie. "Anything people call her to her face starts getting the silence stuck to it. Someone *really* wanted her to be forgotten."

"We need to get to breakfast," said Emily. "It's your first day, and they won't be happy if we're late. I just wanted to ask about your door and thank Cora."

"Thank me? For what?"

"People don't stand up for each other around here. It's not safe."

"If we wanted safe, we wouldn't have gone through the door in the first place," said Sumi. She loosened the tie on her uniform and flashed the other girls a winsome smile. "Let's go. Maybe we'll get ice cream sundaes for our breakfast."

They did not get ice cream for breakfast.

Cora got her expected eggs and turkey bacon. Emily got real bacon and sliced strawberries, which she looked at with clear and obvious revulsion. Sumi, who had received a bowl of oatmeal, began stealing them one by one, hiding them in her own beige breakfast. Stephanie received an actual omelet, oozing with cheese, which she pushed away untouched.

"Look," she whispered, nodding to a table on the other side of the room. "They let her out."

Cora glanced in the direction Stephanie indicated. Her glance became a stare as she realized what she was looking *at*.

Regan was back at the table where she'd eaten breakfast every day since Cora's enrollment in the school. Her head was bowed and her shoulders were slumped, but she was *there*, not locked away in solitary or hidden in some cavern of punishment. There wasn't a single piece of vegetable matter on her plate. It was all bacon, ham, and cheese, worked into a complicated scramble that would probably taste more like butter and grease than anything else.

No one was talking to her. No one was even *looking* at her.

"Man," said Stephanie admiringly. "She almost pulled it off, too."

"Pulled what off?" asked Sumi blankly.

"Regan almost graduated this morning," said Cora.

"If she'd been able to keep her cool a little longer, she'd be out of here," said Stephanie. "She would have gone home with everyone thinking she was better, and no one would have known otherwise until the day they woke up and she wasn't in her bed anymore. If she'd just stayed calm a little while longer—"

"I heard a rumor that we were going to be allowed to play cricket when the weather turns," said Emily abruptly, voice loud and bright. "Do you think it might be true?"

Sumi blinked, and was about to ask why cricket mattered, when the matron behind her said, in a cool voice, "Spending time on rumors is a waste of yourself and others. Have more pride, Emily."

"I'm sorry, matron," said Emily, looking suitably chastened. "I was just excited by the idea of playing an organized sport during physical education. Running laps isn't as challenging as a good game."

The matron considered this, expression thoughtful. Cora held her breath. Sometimes thoughtful people weren't thinking about what you wanted them to be thinking about. Sometimes thoughtful people were thinking about all the ways you could be punished for daring to question what they knew was true.

The matron smiled. Cora exhaled, struggling to keep it from turning into anything that could be interpreted as a huff or a sigh or any number of other forbidden sounds.

"I don't think cricket would be good for your progress, dear," said the matron. "Too many of the rules depend on chance. But I'll talk to the headmaster about finding something more suitable for you to play. Croquet, perhaps. Finish your breakfasts, girls, it's almost time for class." She turned and walked away, leaving the table staring silently after her.

"*All* games have an element of chance," said Stephanie. "*All* games. That's what makes them games and not, I don't know. Arts and crafts."

"Dance classes don't have an element of chance," said Emily

wistfully. "I wouldn't care about sports if they'd let us have a dance class. I'd take anything. Ballroom, tap, anything."

"Did you go to a dancing world?" asked Sumi.

Emily and Stephanie shushed her in unison. It was like being scolded by a choir of very large snakes. Sumi cocked her head and considered them more closely.

Emily was a beautiful girl: anyone with eyes could have seen that. She would have been even lovelier if she'd been allowed to choose her own clothes, dressing in colors that were more flattering to the darkness of her skin, and hair, and eyes than the drab Whitethorn uniforms. She carried herself like a dancer.

Stephanie was an almost perfect contrast, so pale Sumi could see the veins moving beneath her skin like serpentine bruises, dark and harsh and somehow delicate. They all kept their blood under the surface like that, but most of them hid it a little better. Stephanie's hair was swan's-down white, cropped close to her head and lying flat as a cap of feathers, like she might peel it off and toss it away at any moment. Even her eyes were pale, gray-blue trending into white, until it seemed they might bleach entirely into nondescription at any moment.

She *didn't* move like a dancer. She was frail, fragile, but she moved like a bruiser, like she was constantly challenging the world to a fight, and had no doubt that she'd be the winner when it finally agreed to throw down.

"Don't stare," snapped the girl without a name. Sumi glared at her.

"Who do you think you are, the headmaster?" she asked, in a jeering tone.

The headmaster didn't usually come to breakfast. He was content to leave their daily care to the matrons and instructors and each other; someone must have shown him a bucket of crabs at some point early in his academic career, pointing to the way they would police themselves, pulling down any individual who looked too close to breaking free and escaping. "Leave the crabs in the bucket and they'll take care of the rest" seemed to be his philosophy where the student body was concerned.

The girl without a name smiled a small, mean smile and leaned a little closer to Rowena, whispering something in her companion's ear. Rowena giggled, hiding it behind her hand like that would somehow make it less obvious. Cora bristled, and didn't say anything. None of the matrons were approaching. They seemed to have a sixth sense for the difference between camaraderie and bullying. The first, they squelched as quickly as possible. The second, they all but encouraged. A student body preoccupied with eating itself alive was a student body that wasn't making trouble for the administration.

"It's not polite to whisper about people," said Cora.

"I'm closer to graduation than you are," said the girl.

"That just makes you a better liar. You still can't lie and say something's your name when it's not," snapped Cora, and immediately felt bad about it as the girl paled and shrank away. She was a hero. Everyone in the Trenches knew it, even if the people here treated her like a juvenile delinquent who couldn't be trusted with a pair of safety scissors. Heroes weren't supposed to be bullies.

But then, she supposed she wasn't the only hero at the Whitethorn Institute. Most of the children she'd met from the other side of the doors were heroes, in their own specific ways. Maybe heroes *could* be bullies, if they were scared enough. If they were trapped enough. If the sides weren't clear.

How could you choose good over evil when no one was really sure what evil *was*? Under enough pressure, the only good that counted was saving yourself.

Rowena clutched the nameless girl's shoulder with one

hand and glared at Cora, imperious and cold as a queen. "At least she's trying," she snapped. "At least she wants to be better. You say you do, but you keep dyeing your hair. You're going to flunk, and then we're never going to have to look at your stupid face ever again. Come on," and her lips moved in soundless static, unreadable. A brief look of despair washed across her face. Whatever private name she'd been using for the girl she now tugged off the cafeteria bench had clearly reached the end of its usefulness: the strange magic surrounding the nameless girl had recognized it, and so it, like everything else, had been washed away.

Cora watched them go before glancing back to Emily and Stephanie, a frown on her face and a question in her eyes. "What happens if you flunk? Regan sabotaged her own graduation, and she's still here." Maybe flunking meant the same thing as expulsion. Maybe she could be thrown back to the Drowned Gods if she didn't try harder.

"We don't know," said Stephanie. "No one does."

Sumi frowned. "Oh," she said. "That probably means it isn't good."

Emily nodded, expression grave. Then she leaned forward, opened her mouth, and said, "But I heard—"

Whatever she'd heard was cut off by the bell ringing to signal the end of breakfast. Cora rose with the others, automatically gathering the detritus of both her meal and Sumi's, stacking the trays neatly and efficiently. The Logic girls left their dishes strewn willy-nilly across their tables, some of them looking back at the mess with clear agony in their eyes, like leaving things out of place was causing them active pain. The oatmeal girls put their own trays on the busing station, then moved to clean up after the waffle girls, Nonsense children making order out of the chaos left behind by the Logicians.

Sumi twitched like she was going to start scavenging the abandoned waffles. Cora reacted without thinking, clamping her hand around Sumi's wrist.

"No," she hissed. "A matron will see you."

"But—"

"No," echoed Stephanie. "We're your dormmates. We'll teach you the rules."

Emily was waiting at the door. Sumi only glanced back once as Cora dragged her to the other member of their sudden alliance, and then they were moving into the hall, merging smoothly with the tide of students. By the time the bell rang again, the hallway was empty, and the Whitethorn Institute was at peace.

9 MICE IN THE WALLS

THE CLASSROOM MIGHT AS well have been a medical exam room, or a cardboard box exaggerated beyond all reason. The walls were devoid of anything, even educational posters or homework charts; the fluorescent lights had no covers, and hummed quietly to themselves as they illuminated the barren, institutional desks and their solemn, empty-handed occupants. No one drew on the desktops or used their protractors to etch initials into the wood: no one even breathed without permission from the matron at the front of the room, who was droning on about the history of the world, pausing occasionally to remind them that *this* was the only history that mattered, *this* was the only history that could be believed in.

It took most of Sumi's attention to keep herself from interrupting, pointing out how it was funny how "real" history seemed to be all about white men doing important things while everyone else barely existed except when they needed to be shown the errors of their ways. It made sense that the self-made heroes would have written history to make them look as good as possible. It didn't make sense for everyone else to be expected to believe it. It was like saying water was dry and the sky was red, and somehow making that the law of the land.

Sometimes she felt like the world where she'd been born was the most nonsensical of them all. Sure, gravity always worked and clouds didn't talk, but people told lies big enough to block the sun, and everyone just *let* them, like it was nothing to revise the story of an entire world to make yourself feel better.

Cora sat next to her, hands folded, attention on the teacher. Sumi tried to study her without being obvious about it. The rainbows on her skin were faded, almost gone, and the blue-green of her hair had lost some of its impossible luster. She looked more like a girl with a questionable dye job than a mermaid. Sumi wanted to be angry at her. This was what she'd *wanted,* somehow. This was what she'd been looking for.

All she succeeded in feeling was tired. Tired of this place, tired of Cora's trauma; she'd barely been at Whitethorn for an hour, and she already felt overwhelmed and exhausted. This place was a vampire. It would drain her dry if she let it.

The school was built like a fortress, thick-walled, forbidding. From what she'd seen so far, the doors were alarmed; when someone opened one of them without first entering the correct code, they would screech and raise a ruckus, making any quiet exit impossible. Most of the windows were bolted shut. The few that *did* open had bars bolted to their frames, and not even Sumi could wiggle her way between them. If she *had* been able to, she wouldn't have been able to get down; none of the windows below the second floor were on the list of possible escapes.

Even Antoinette hadn't been able to find blueprints for the building online, and there were no convenient widow's walks or bits of decorative moulding. It was like the people who'd designed this school had never read a single story that depended entirely on a heroic escape.

Or maybe they'd read them all, and used that knowledge to build the perfect academic mousetrap, capable of containing the perfect academic mice.

The grounds were no better. The wall Sumi and Cora had

both seen on their way in circled the entire property, lined on the inside with razor wire and electrically charged mesh that hadn't been visible from the road. Touching the stone meant drawing blood, taking a shock, or both. Cora had seen a dead deer hanging off the wall during one of her physical education nature walks. Its antlers had been tangled in the wire, and its eyes had been gone, replaced by hollow craters.

"That's why we don't touch the wall, children," the matron leading the group had said.

The matron at the front of the room paused, looking at Sumi expectantly. Sumi realized, heart sinking, that she'd been asked a question without hearing a single word—and more, that everyone in the room was looking at her. Some, like Emily and Stephanie, were sympathetic. Others, like Rowena and the girl without a name, were on the verge of gloating, clearly delighted by her predicament.

Sometimes the only way out was through. Sumi sat up straighter, tilted her head to the side, and asked, in an utterly guileless tone, "What was the question again?"

"Do you think woolgathering is the best use of your time, Miss Onishi?" asked the matron. "You'll be expected to rejoin the real world as a functional adult soon enough, and this sort of behavior will not be tolerated."

"I know plenty of functional adults who do a lot worse than staring off into space, and no one punishes *them*," said Sumi. "Why do you keep calling this the real world when you know it's not the only world there is? Is this a 'no other gods before me' somehow turning into monotheism situation? Because I didn't agree to go to seminary school. I'd make a terrible nun. No one would ever listen to any scripture I tried to share, and then we'd all wind up frustrated and probably start throwing things at each other. Better not to start, don't you think?"

The silence that filled the classroom was so profound that Sumi could hear the blood rushing in her ears, a soothing personal ocean slowly pulling her away from the shore.

Moving deliberately, the matron put down her eraser.

"Miss Onishi, you're new here, and I think you misunderstand your role at this school," she said, voice stiff and diction precise. "You're not here to argue with adults. You're not here to confuse your peers. You're here to learn from them. You're here to be *better*."

"Better than what, though?" asked Sumi. "You know this world isn't the only one." It seemed suddenly important, suddenly essential, that she get the matron to admit that. "The headmaster said so when he let me into the school. You *know* the doors are real. You know it's all real. So why?"

The matron opened her mouth to reply. Then she caught herself, and really looked at Sumi, and she *smiled*.

It was a terrible thing, that smile. It was filled with shadows more dangerous than any wicked queen, more deadly than any sword, and Sumi drew away from it, as far as the limits of her chair would allow.

"Class, we're very fortunate today; we're witnessing a breakthrough in our newest student," said the matron. "We know the doors exist, because every one of us has had an encounter with them. We'd be fools to pretend they weren't threats. But that doesn't mean we have to grant them the privilege of becoming 'real.' Miss Carlton, what is 'real'?"

"Real is something you can see and touch and take comfort in," said Emily, in a lilting, artificially high voice, like she was trying to make sure every syllable was perfect.

"Is a dream real?"

"While you're sleeping, it can seem that way," said Emily. "But when you wake up, your bed, that's real. The morning sunlight, that's real. The dream just . . . goes away, back where it belongs."

"What would happen if you refused to let go of your dream? Anyone?"

The girl without a name put her hand up. The matron nodded to her, and she said, in a tight, piping voice, "You'd die. You'd starve while you were sleeping, or you'd get an infection from bedsores, or you'd just stop breathing. You can't be a person and live in dreams."

"So dreams can be dangerous, if you treat them like nourishment."

The nameless girl looked to Emily, who nodded. Her face was pinched, and there was a hectic brightness in her eyes that spoke, silently, of tears. The matron ignored the signs of discontent in order to focus on Sumi.

"If a parent tells a child that something is poison, that something isn't good food, is it the place of the child to argue, or to listen? After all, the parent knows more. The parent has had more time to learn the ways the world can destroy something delicate and lovely."

"You're not my parent," said Sumi. "They're dead. Both of them. You'd have to be a corpse, and maybe then you wouldn't be lecturing me on whether dreams are real things or not. My door isn't a dream."

"It isn't a dream, but it isn't good food, either," said the matron. "We are here, in this wonderful place, because we went through a door and into a world that shouldn't have been there, a world that wasn't good for us. You must not look at goblin men, you must not buy their fruit. A very wise woman said that. What do you think she meant?"

"I knew a woman who'd been to the Goblin Market, and she always said Rossetti was a well-intentioned hack," said Sumi.

"She died after I did. I guess she's stayed that way, though, or she'd probably be here too, and we could all be miserable together."

"Sumi, hush," hissed Cora.

"You know she's telling lies," said Sumi. "You know you're a mermaid. I'm sorry you felt like you had to run away to be safe, but no one gets to dry you out for their own sake. No one gets to hurt you like this."

The matron's lips pressed together into a thin, bloodless line. "We aren't here to hurt you, Miss Onishi. We're here to prepare you to live in the world where you were born. We're here to teach you how to *survive*."

"Died once, didn't like it, not going to do it again," said Sumi. "There. That's survival. Can I go home now?"

"You can go to the headmaster's office," said the matron. She pointed to the door. "Now. Miss Miller will escort you there."

Sumi rose. Her legs wanted to shake and her knees wanted to knock together and she didn't let them. She was proud of that.

Cora rose less gracefully, face so pale that she looked like she was going to be sick. She walked to the door, waiting there for Sumi to catch up.

Together, the two girls walked out of the room, leaving the well-lit, oppressive classroom for the dim, equally oppressive hall.

More rooms lined the hallway than could possibly be in current use. Cora didn't have a clear idea of the size of the student body—they were kept too isolated from one another, aside from mealtime and classes—but she was sure it was less than three hundred, which still made it considerably larger than Eleanor's school. The matrons liked to imply that the majority of the students were voluntary enrollments, yearning to forget the weight that had been placed upon their shoulders by the worlds they'd been called upon to save. Cora wasn't sure she believed them.

Rowena might be a voluntary enrollment. Cora still had no idea what kind of world the other girl had gone to, but from the way Rowena sometimes woke up screaming and clawing at the air, she was pretty sure it hadn't been a pleasant one. And the girl without a name, she was voluntary. She had said so.

They walked, and the sound of their footsteps in their hard-soled, sensible shoes was like the tapping of a typewriter's keys, strong and regular. Cora looked at Sumi crossly.

"You didn't have to come here," she said. "I'm here to save myself, not because I wanted someone to save me."

"Heroism is addictive. Maybe that's why it sounds so much like 'heroin.'"

"Maybe," agreed Cora. "But I'm fixing it. I'm breaking the Drowned Gods' hold on me." She flexed her rainbow-hued hands. "I'll be free soon."

"But at what cost?" asked Sumi softly.

Cora didn't have an answer.

The sound of someone else breathing slipped into the space between their footfalls. Sumi slowed down, gesturing for Cora to do the same. Whoever it was wasn't just breathing: they were crying, the sound soft and thin and pained. Sumi worried her lip momentarily between her teeth. Then she turned and followed the sound, working her way down the hall until she came to a door that had been left ever so slightly ajar.

Holding her breath to keep herself from making a sound, Sumi pressed her eye against the opening and peered through. There was a classroom, virtually identical to the one she'd just been ejected from, but there was no class, no matron: just a single teenage girl in a Whitethorn uniform, her hands pressed over her face to muffle the sound of her sobbing.

She was tall, or would have been, if she'd been standing, with the kind of broad shoulders that came from a childhood spent doing heavy labor, layering muscle over muscle. Her hair was dark blonde, the color of old hay, and like Sumi's, had been tamed into a braid. Also like Sumi's, it was doing its best to escape, breaking free in wisps and irrepressible curls, until it looked like a dandelion on the verge of going to seed.

Cora gasped, the sound small and quickly stifled. Regan was enough of a recognizable figure around the school that seeing her face wasn't necessary.

Lingering in this empty classroom, talking to this crying girl, would make them late reaching the headmaster's office. The cameras would have picked them up by now, and would know the path she was supposed to be taking. There were cameras everywhere except the bathrooms, even in the dorm rooms where they slept, making privacy as much of a longed-for dream as rainbows and fires and the flight of the moon mantas. Once they were late, they'd be in trouble. Once they were in trouble, almost anything could happen, and very little of it would be anything they'd enjoy.

Cora knew she should hurry Sumi along, and leave Regan for someone else to find. But she'd already been a bully once today, and if she walked away from Regan while she was crying, if she left Regan alone, maybe she wouldn't be able to call herself a hero anymore. Maybe this was where she got to choose.

"Be sure," she whispered to herself, and stepped into the classroom with Sumi at her heels, easing the door shut behind them.

The latch clicked softly when it snapped home. Regan froze, her last sob transforming into a strangled, agonized squeaking sound. Cora winced. She was making things worse. She seemed to have a talent for it here, in this school, where there were too many rules and none of them understood what it was to be merciful.

"I'm made of candy," said Sumi.

Regan slowly lowered her hands and turned, staring at Sumi. She had a wide, friendly face, the sort of face that belonged on the other side of a breakfast table, smiling and happy and ready to face the day. It didn't deserve to be miserable and streaked with tears. That wasn't *fair*.

"What?" she asked.

"Candy. I'm made of candy. Technically I think that makes me a really fancy doll, since people are supposed to be made of meat. Only I'm made of meat, too, because the Baker baked me back into being a girl, instead of a kind of pastry, so I bleed and stuff, and I guess I can probably die again. I haven't tried it." Sumi cocked her head and smiled, as encouragingly as she could. "Okay. Your turn."

Regan blinked slowly. "I . . . what?"

"I just said something big and ridiculous and impossible that can't possibly be so. Now it's your turn to say something big and ridiculous and impossible. I want you to believe me, so I'll believe you, and then we'll be friends, because friends believe each other. It's your turn."

Regan stared at her for a moment, eyes wide and wet and a little bit wild, like she was thinking of running away, like she was thinking of escape. She shifted her gaze to Cora.

Cora shrugged. "I'm a mermaid."

Finally, slowly, Regan said, "I can talk to horses."

"All horses, or only special horses?"

"Only special horses at first, but . . ." Regan hesitated. "There was a door."

Sumi nodded encouragement. She wanted to rush the other girl, wanted to remind her that there was always a door someplace where a door wasn't supposed to be, there was always a sign saying to be sure, there was always a choice. They didn't have much time before the matrons realized they were missing and started flicking through the camera feeds, and then . . .

The punishment for this was going to be enormous. Sumi rejoiced, because when they got punished, they were going to be punished for *doing* something, not just for being who they were and not who the adults around them wanted them to be. *Doing* was always better than just being. *Doing* was a choice.

"I didn't mean to go through," said Regan. "I knew it wasn't right, a door being where a door wasn't supposed to be—where a door *couldn't* be. Who puts a door next to a creek? It's silly. It doesn't make sense. But it was there, and I was so alone, and I thought, what can it hurt? No one's going to miss me. And then, on the other side, I could talk to . . . not horses, because there weren't *horses* there, not really, but anything with hooves; and anything with hooves could talk to me. They all *wanted* to talk to me. And they were such amazing things. Centaurs and hippogriffs and beasts like horses but with all kinds of different wings, and kelpies and silenes and it was . . . it was home, you know? I went home. I finally knew where home *was,* and it was so good, and I was so happy."

"And then you found another door, and you wound up where you'd been in the beginning, but now you knew there was something better out there, and it was like trying to go back to nothing but oatmeal after you'd finally tasted cake," said Sumi sympathetically. She was snipping off the tail of Regan's story and she felt bad about that, she honestly did. Time was running out. "We haven't met before. I'm Sumi. You were on the morning announcements. You didn't get to go home. Why didn't you get to go home?"

"Because if I'd lied to that many people, I don't think I would ever have been able to be sure I deserved to go back," said Regan. "I want to go back. More than anything, I want to go back. I don't want to be here—I hate it here—but I miss my home."

Cora frowned. Had she been doing the same thing herself, all this time? What made lying different when she did it? Did denying the Drowned Gods mean she was no longer worthy of the Trenches?

Sumi nodded, quick and tight and understanding. "Your world isn't Nonsense, is it?"

"Nonsense?"

Cora sighed. "They call it 'Delusion' here."

"Oh," said Regan. "Um, no. I didn't go to a Delusional world. I went to a Compulsion world."

"Logic," said Sumi, satisfied. "That makes sense. I bet if I cut one of your horses open, they'd have different throats."

"Please don't cut any horses open," said Regan. "I don't think it's their throats. I think it's my ears, because a week after I came back to the house where I grew up, I got to go riding on my old mare again, and I could understand every word she said. She's not a really good conversationalist—she mostly talks about food and where she itches and how much she wants another apple—but I know what she's saying, and no one around me does."

"Ears, brain, what a pain." Sumi glanced at the camera in the corner of the classroom. Was it her imagination, or was the lens pointed at them? "How did you get here all by yourself? During my orientation, they told me we were never supposed to be all by ourselves."

"I was supposed to go home today," said Regan. "They didn't know what to do with me after they sent my parents away. They already pulled me out of all my classes. So the matron told me to sit here and think about how much I've disappointed everyone who was counting on me to get better."

"Okay," said Sumi. "Okay. I have to hit you now."

Regan recoiled. "What?"

Cora blinked. "What?"

"The cameras watch but I bet they don't *listen*, I think they don't have the people to listen, so they can see us, you and me talking, but they don't know what we're saying to each other. They won't blame you if they think I'm the one who started it. I want to talk to you more. If they think you want that, too, they'll never let us be alone anywhere together, ever again. So I have to hit you now. Okay?"

Regan looked like this was anything but "okay": like this was, in fact, the worst idea ever voiced in her presence. But she was easily half again Sumi's size, and there was no question of who would win if they got into a real fight; she wasn't in any danger. So slowly, reluctantly, she nodded.

"Okay," she said.

Sumi moved faster than seemed possible, moved with the speed that had carried her across the Candy Cane Fields and seen her the sole survivor of the Battle of Gingerbread Gorge. Her hand lashed out, catching Regan squarely across the face, and if it was more sound than actual impact, it didn't matter, because Regan toppled over anyway. To the cameras, her surprise would look like pain and fear. Cora danced back, away from the spray of blood from Regan's nose. Cameras could lie even when they told the exact truth, because cameras couldn't record everything. Only the surface.

"Find me when you can," whispered Sumi, and turned, running out of the room as hard and fast as she could. Her shoes were too heavy. They slowed her down. She did the math in her head, measured the temporary delay against the loss over time, and turned her run into an awkward hop, untying the laces of her school shoes and kicking them away, then yanking off her socks, leaving them discarded in the middle of the hall.

The feel of tile against her bare feet was rejuvenating. She laughed with the sheer joy of it all, untying her tie as she ran for the distant shadow of the exit. The buttons on her shirt were next, and then the buttons on her skirt, layer following layer until she was running naked down the middle of the hall, hair streaming behind her, adrenaline and cold tightening her skin, making it feel like her own again.

A matron stepped out of the shadows next to the door, wrapping an arm around Sumi's middle so tightly that the air was knocked out of the smaller, girl, leaving her gasping, still laughing, drowning gleefully on dry land. She kept laughing as she was hauled away, as she was slung into the plain white room of solitary to think about what she'd done.

They might not be going home, but they weren't going to stay here. Sumi was sure of it.

Eventually, her laughter burned itself out. It was a sudden blaze, not a sustained bonfire; it could never have lasted. She curled up in a corner of the plain white room, tucking her arm under her head, and fell into an uneasy doze.

But Cora: ah, Cora. Cora had always been a runner, and this time, she didn't run. She helped Regan back to her chair and stood, placidly silent, until the matrons came and dragged her to a plain white room of her own. Eventually, she fell asleep, and there were no shadows here, no corners for the Drowned Gods to claim and colonize.

She was dreaming of the open sea when a sudden shock of

icy water splashed across her face. She sat bolt upright, clutching the thin blanket she'd been given around herself.

The headmaster looked down at her, the empty glass still held in one hand, and shook his head. "You were doing so well, Cora," he said. "What in the world made you stand by while your friend assaulted another student?"

"She made us late to breakfast," said Cora. "You always say punctuality is a virtue, and she made us less virtuous. So when Sumi hit her, I didn't stop her. Instead, I did what you said and turned my back on weakness."

"And why did you barge into a room where you had no business being, when you were meant to be escorting Miss Onishi to my office?"

"We heard—I mean—" Cora stopped, trapped between her pretense of turning her back on weakness and admitting her sympathy for Regan.

"I see." The headmaster nodded slightly, seeming to read her thoughts in the same way he had seemed to on her first day. "I hope you understand that I am very disappointed in you."

Cora bit the inside of her cheek. The headmaster's disappointment was like a chain around her throat, dragging her down to where the Drowned Gods still waited, singing their poisonous songs. Desperately, she blurted out, "Where is Regan? Where is Sumi?"

"Miss Lewis and Miss Onishi are spending time in quiet contemplation while we review their respective educational plans," he replied with a cold smile. "They may each require a bit more . . . specialized help in the future."

"No!" Cora couldn't stop herself; she couldn't stand to pretend anymore. "Can't you see that you're hurting people? Don't you care?"

"Did you forget why you came here, Miss Miller? The singing of the sea in your ears? The rainbows on your skin?" The headmaster grabbed her wrist, turning it so that her palm faced the ceiling. "They've faded, but they haunt you still. How could I allow you to leave before they disappear? How could any caring guardian allow their students to continue carrying the weight of such a delusion?"

Cora shook him off. "I'm a student. Not a prisoner. I refuse to trade one monster for another."

"If we're monsters, so is Miss West."

Cora went very still.

The headmaster smiled, almost sympathetically. "We're sister schools. One can't exist without the other. Yes, we have our share of involuntary enrollments—but really, how many of the students at your last school were consulted before they were shipped away by parents who no longer understood them? How many of them got to choose? You think of Miss West fondly because she gave you what you wanted to have, she told you what you wanted to hear. We're as much on your side as she ever was."

"I came to you voluntarily," said Cora. "Regan didn't. You're not setting her free. You're hurting her."

"It's true that Miss Lewis never had the benefit of choosing her education. But your Miss West never taught you how to fit into this world, either. She let you wallow in regret, knowing that most doors never reappear. Her way, my way, it doesn't matter. You're part of this world now, Cora. You're not going back to your underwater fantasyland. You were a hero, and now that's done, and you're a teenage girl again. You need to learn to live with that. Someone has to teach you."

"I didn't ask you to teach me," said Cora. "I asked you to free me."

The headmaster smiled that terrifying smile. "But you did, Miss Miller. You asked me to teach you how to forget. You enrolled here because you wanted to forget the monsters, and you will, oh yes, you will. You have so much more to learn before you leave us. I'll free you from your gods and monsters. *All* of them."

"You . . . you *are* a monster," said Cora, almost wonderingly. "You're hurting the people you say you're trying to help. You're a monster in a hall of heroes, and we're going to defeat you. That's what heroes do. We beat monsters, no matter how much it costs us."

"But that's what I've been trying to tell you," said the headmaster, crossing to the door and opening it with a simple twist of his wrist, like it was nothing, like freedom was a toy. "You're not heroes anymore. Not here. It's time for you to accept that you aren't going to win. This is a world without heroes, and you're here."

Then he was gone, and Cora was alone. More alone than she had ever been before.

She put her hands over her face, and she cried.

PART III

THE DOORS THAT OPEN, THE DOORS THAT CLOSE

10 A CROWBAR OR A KEY

THE DROWNED GODS CAME for her as soon as she fell asleep.

They came as she had seen them in the Moors, unspeakable towers of tentacled flesh, suckers pulsing, surfaces bristling with eyes in a thousand shades of sunset, their pupils like sine curves against fields of red and gold and pink.

"You belong to us, little mermaid," they whispered. "We gave you back your legs. We gave you back your voice. You belong to *us*."

"I do not." In dreams, Cora had her fins and her scales again, and the lashing of her tail held her upright, as freed from the bonds of gravity as the Drowned Gods themselves. "I fell because you designed the bridge to fall. An animal that falls into a trap may be caught, but that doesn't make it a possession."

"We flushed you out of hiding. You are ours."

"I am not. I refuse." The water was sweet. Cora inhaled deeply. "The gods of the Trenches and the gods of the Moors aren't the same. You don't belong in these currents. Be gone."

"Not alone." A tentacle lashed out, wrapping tight around her waist, trying to drag her forward. Cora shook her head, silently refusing to be moved, and try as the Drowned God might, it couldn't budge her. She hung in the sea like a star.

"I will not," she said. "I am not yours to cling to or claim. Go back to your own waters."

Her time at the Whitethorn Institute had weakened their

hold on her. She knew that now. In the months of resisting Whitethorn's pressure to transform her into something else, she had somehow built up her strength to resist the Drowned Gods' attempts to do the same thing. And their desperation was growing, or they wouldn't have approached her so directly. She was stronger than they were, here in this familiar sea.

Slowly, the tentacle unwound from her waist. "We will be back."

"And I will not go with you. Now, or ever. This is not your place." She took another breath. "I am not your door."

The eyes of the Drowned Gods slammed shut, taking the light they had cast with them, leaving Cora alone in the dark water. She floated in place, arms spread, hair a skirl around her face. To the silence she repeated:

"I am not your door." After a pause for thought, she added, "But I might be my own."

Cora sighed, and stretched, and woke in a cold, white-walled room with a thin blanket wrapped around her legs, binding them together into a child's approximation of a tail. She kicked once, enjoying the way her industrial cotton "flukes" bounced, and waited for someone to come and let her out.

It was several hours later when she stepped into the dorm room, a matron behind her and her eyes pointed at the floor, so she wouldn't have to look at any of the people in the room. She was back in her uniform, her hair perfectly combed and pulled back in a neat French twist that wouldn't have looked out of place in a senior portrait.

"Please remind Miss Miller of how we do things around here," said the matron. "I trust you can be gentle with her." She stepped out of the room without waiting for an answer, closing the door as she went.

Sumi, seated cross-legged on her bed, didn't move.

Emily gasped. "Cora, your *hair . . .*"

"I know. Pretty, isn't it?" Cora lifted her head, smiling like a shark's fin cutting through still water. There were no rainbows left on her skin. They had all flowed into her hair, which was still blue-green, but now gleamed nacre-iridescent and impossible.

"You've been gone for three days," said Sumi. Her voice was flat. "They only kept me for one."

"It didn't feel like three days to me," said Cora. "I was dreaming for most of it."

Sumi nodded as if this made perfect sense. "Did they feed you?"

The nameless girl scoffed from her place on the other side of the room. "Of course they fed her. This is a school, not a prison."

"No," snapped Emily. The nameless girl flinched, looking startled. "For *you* it's a school, because you want to be here. The rules are different for people who enrolled voluntarily. They're not afraid you're going to run. This *is* a prison. You're just lucky enough not to be able to see the bars."

"I enrolled voluntarily," said Cora. "But no, they didn't feed me."

"Not like you needed it," said the nameless girl, forcing the sneer back onto her face like she thought no one would have noticed when it disappeared.

"I bet you'd fit under the bathroom sink," said Emily pleasantly. "You wouldn't have a month ago, but now? You look like you're just the right size."

The nameless girl paled, clapping a hand over her mouth like she was going to be sick. Then she bolted from the room, presumably heading for the bathroom. Rowena lowered her book and gave Emily a reproachful look.

"That wasn't kind," she said.

"*She* isn't kind," said Emily. "It's not my fault if she can't take what she dishes out."

Cora started laughing.

Rowena looked at her with disgust. "No food for three days, rainbows in her hair, and now she's laughing? She's dangerous."

"She can hear you," said Emily.

"Maybe." Rowena leaned back against her pillows. "If she starts screaming for no reason, you'll have to get rid of her. I need my sleep."

"You're a monster," snapped Emily.

"That's why I'm here," said Rowena, and went back to her book.

"Why did they keep you for three days?" asked Sumi.

Cora kept laughing.

"They wouldn't have hurt her, would they?" asked Emily, a nervous edge in her voice. "They're not supposed to hurt us."

"Everything about this place is hurting us," said Stephanie.

Cora choked on her laughter and stopped, falling silent. A single tear ran down her cheek. Like her hair, it was full of rainbows. "I enrolled here voluntarily, but we have to leave," she said.

Sumi threw her hands up. "Thank the Baker! Now how do we get out of here?"

The door opened. The door closed. The nameless girl leaned against it, putting one more barrier between them and the outside world, and said, "You don't."

"Why don't you go stuff yourself in a hole?" Emily never

took her eyes off Cora. "Sumi, you can't help her plan an escape attempt. She'll just get us all hurt."

Rowena slid off the bed, skirting the little knot of damaged, damaging girls to stand next to the nameless girl. "I'm going to get a matron," she said.

Surprisingly, it was the nameless girl who said, "No, you're not."

Rowena turned to stare at her. The nameless girl shook her head.

"The matrons can't help. If you go to get one now, we'll all be in trouble." The nameless girl moved so that she was standing almost nose-to-nose with Cora. Taking a deep breath, she said, "Be ready to grab Rowena."

"But—"

"Do it." She looked Cora dead in the eye, and said, "My name is—"

The sound that came out of her mouth wasn't nothingness, wasn't blankness. It was static loud enough to drown out the world. It was the howling of the limitless void between universes, and when it was over, Cora blinked, expression going thoughtful as she took a step backward.

"Oh," she said.

"It was my own fault," said the nameless girl. "I thought I could handle it."

"We all make mistakes," said Cora. She turned to Emily, and a flicker of regret crossed her face. "I'm sorry. I didn't mean to frighten you all."

"I still don't get why they held you for three days," said Stephanie. "Sumi's the one who hit Regan, and she came back days ago. Why didn't you?"

"I yelled at the headmaster," said Cora.

Everything was silent for a long beat, before Sumi said,

"Listen. I was dead once. It hurt. It wasn't anything, and it hurt anyway, because death doesn't need to be something to hurt. And then I went to a whole bunch of different places, pulled apart like taffy, and *that* didn't hurt until I was together again. It hurts now when I dream. I fought in a war and I won and I lived, and I buried my parents and I broke my brother's heart and I lived, and I died because a scared child wanted to go home, and I didn't blame her, because I might have done the same thing if I'd been in her petticoats. She was trying to be clever the only way she knew how."

Emily looked at her blankly. "Why does that matter?"

"Because the people here think they're helping us. They think they're heroes and we're monsters, and because they believe it all the way down to the base of them, they can do almost anything and feel like they're doing the right thing." Sumi rubbed her wrist, almost idly. "They can lock someone in a white room where the light never goes off and say it's because they can't have any more illusions. They can not feed you but give you lots of water and no toilet, and say it's because the real world doesn't always meet your needs. They can do a lot of things. This isn't a good place. Even if you're here because you want to be, this isn't a good place. This place *hurts* people. It makes them crawl into their own hearts to be safe, and then it turns those hearts against them."

There was so much more she could have said, like the way the war was still echoing in her ears, the way she could hear the screams of the wounded and the weeping of the captured. She could have told them about the wisps she wasn't sure were memories, the little fragments of the Halls of the Dead, her voice hollow and stolen from her mouth, her hands motionless by her intangible sides. Most of all, she could have told them about Sumiko, poor shade, discarded self, who was stirring more and more, because Sumi had been the necessary armor to survive Confection, and Sumiko was the necessary armor to survive the Whitethorn Institute.

She could have. She didn't. The words were too much and would have distracted from the only thing that mattered.

"We can't stay here," she said. "They'll devour us if we stay."

"Well, *I'm* not leaving," said Rowena. "They hurt you because you wouldn't listen. You wouldn't follow the rules. The rest of us don't have your problems."

For a long moment, the room was completely silent.

"I am," said the nameless girl.

All four of the others turned to look at her. Her cheeks reddened.

"I came here because my parents said it would help me," she said. "I've done everything I was asked to do. I've followed all the rules, even the ones that don't make sense, and for what? I'm still shrinking. I still don't have a name. Anything that *starts* to feel like a name disappears. Maybe I'm doomed, but I'd rather be doomed in my own room, with my own things around me, than be doomed here, where they make me eat shredded wheat for breakfast and peanut butter sandwiches for lunch and act like cheese is the root of all evils. I want to go home."

The longing in her voice was complicated and undeniable. She might not know where home was anymore, but she knew she wanted to be there. She knew she wanted to wrap it around herself and let it carry her away.

"You'll never get better if you run," said Rowena.

"I'm not getting better now," said the nameless girl. She looked earnestly at Rowena. "We're friends, aren't we? We've always been friends. I've never asked you for anything. Well, I'm asking you for something now."

"I'm not running away from school," said Rowena. "I came here because this is where I need to be."

"You don't have run away," said the nameless girl. "You just have to promise not to tell on us when we do."

"I want . . . I want this to matter, but it doesn't," said Emily. "You understand that, don't you? No matter how much we want to leave, we can't. The doors are locked. The grounds are walled in. We're all being watched, and that goes double for Cora. We're here until we graduate, or until our families take us home."

"That won't happen," said Rowena.

Sumi looked at her curiously. She shrugged.

"My first dormmate was this weird kid who liked to say math was negotiable and she could do the calculus at the heart of the universe if we'd give her some chalk. She wrote her parents every week, asking them to take her home. She said all the right things. But they never came for her, and when she finally graduated, her dad said something about how all that silence had been worth it if it meant they got their daughter back. Don't you understand? They never saw her letters. The matrons control the mail, and the headmaster controls the matrons, and if he doesn't want us talking to anyone on the outside, we won't. There's no rescue coming. You're here until you graduate. That's the only way out."

"And you still don't want to leave?" asked Cora.

Rowena shook her head. "I like it here. I like the rules and the structure and waking up every day knowing the air will be breathable and the water won't be. I don't enjoy having the laws of physics treated like a game of red rover, okay? Some kids get magical worlds full of sunshine and laughter. Me, I got 'the floor is lava' from a place that really meant it. I could graduate tomorrow if I wanted to. But out there, in the real world, doors can pop out of nowhere and sweep you away. Out there, the rules can *change*."

"Huh." Cora looked around the room, assessing every line and angle. "You're right."

"What?" asked Rowena.

"The rules never change in here. The rules never change at *all*." Cora turned back to Rowena. "Be sure. That's what all the doors say. Everyone I've talked to—and people at my old school talked a *lot*—has said that. Be sure, and if you are, wonderful things can happen to you. Be sure. If I was ever sure in my life, I was sure when in that room, when I told the Drowned Gods I didn't belong to them. It was my moment of catharsis, and I can't be the only one. This place is like a psychic licorice shop. A hundred flavors of 'sure,' and somehow none of them are enough to bring back the sun, none of them are enough to open a door, for *anyone*? That doesn't make sense. Someone's keeping the doors away."

"The matrons say we have to give up the idea of going back, because it doesn't happen," said Emily uncertainly. "That's part of why it's so important we learn to let go of where we went, what we . . . were. Because even if we don't, we'll never get to go back."

"Lots of people go back," said Sumi. She waved a hand, like she was trying to brush away a particularly unpleasant smell. "Not everyone. Most people can't be entirely sure they'd be happier in one place over another, so they don't find their doors again. But lots of people go back. They have the right combination of selfish and lonely and hopeful and stupid and earnest and selfless, and they find their doors, and they go back. There's more students here than there are at Eleanor's. Someone should be able to find their door. If no one can, what does that say?"

"What does it matter what that says?" asked Stephanie. "If they're being locked, they're being locked. We don't have a key."

"Sometimes you don't need a key," said Sumi. Her smile verged on feral. "Sometimes a crowbar is good enough."

"I have a plan, I think," said Cora. "But I'm going to need you to work with me—even you, Rowena. You don't have to come with us, but you have to be on our side."

"What do I get out of it?" asked Rowena.

"We leave," said Cora.

Rowena thought for a moment. Then she nodded. "All right," she said. "What do I have to do?"

11 WHERE THE LOST ONES GO

WHEN THE BELL RANG for breakfast, the girls walked into the cafeteria single file, with Rowena and the nameless girl at the front, followed by Stephanie and Emily, and finally, at the rear, Sumi and Cora. Silence fell over the room, silence so deep and so unbreakable that even the sound of the oatmeal bubbling in its tureen seemed almost offensively loud.

Cora ignored the way people stared as she moved, with quick precision, to take her place in the breakfast line. Her uniform was meticulous, her tie knotted perfectly enough to make a wardrobe master weep. Her hair, sleek and shining and filled with rainbows, was pulled back with two barrettes, keeping it away from her face. There was nothing loose or fluid about her movements; she walked like she had a purpose, and like she was going to accomplish it, come hell or high water.

One of the matrons was the first to recover. She smiled at Cora—the first smile many of the girls had seen on her face—and said, "Good morning, Miss Miller. You're looking well today."

"I feel well today, thank you, matron," said Cora, and even her voice was level and calm. It was the voice of someone who had considered all their options, and come to the conclusion that an early bedtime, a balanced diet, and flossing were the true keys to happiness. "I appreciate your consideration."

The matron nodded, surprise and pleasure still written plainly on her face. "It's always wonderful to witness someone successfully breaking through their troubles. I think you deserve a little reward, to acknowledge such a lovely morning. You may have a spoonful of brown sugar, if you'd like."

Her expression remained pleasant, even mild. The same couldn't be said of the other matrons in the room, whose eyes hardened as they watched Cora to see what her response was going to be.

Cora shook her head. "I appreciate the offer, I really do, but my stomach is still queasy from my past few days of being unwell; it's best if I stick with bland food for the moment." She ladled a healthy portion of oatmeal into a bowl and placed it on her tray, offering the matron a polite smile. "Perhaps to-morrow."

She walked to the table she shared with her dormmates, back straight and shoulders squared, and pretended not to no-tice the approving glances being sent in her direction, or the way some of the students were starting to whisper behind their hands.

The other girls joined her at the table, each with their bland, approved breakfast. Sumi ate her turkey bacon and eggs with small, precise bites, not looking at the plates of waffles in front of the Logic girls, or at the strawberries on Emily's plate. Cora ate as if she thought oatmeal was the most desirable thing in the entire world, worthy of being slowly savored. When she was done, she bused her own dishes, placing them in the ap-propriate basins, before moving to wait by the door for the rest of the girls in her dorm to finish.

Regan watched all this out of the corner of her eye, a look of profound regret on her face. She'd known Sumi would go to solitary for the crime of hitting her, and she'd understood Sumi was taking the blame on her own shoulders to spare Re-gan; of the two of them, it had seemed obvious that Regan was the more fragile. She hadn't expected them to punish Cora as well, or as harshly.

Just before the group walked out of the room, in a moment when the matrons were focused on the students who seemed more in need of their guidance and attention, Cora met Regan's eye and winked. It was a small gesture. By the time Regan processed what it might actually mean, the girls were gone, heading for their first class.

Regan sat alone, surrounded by the girls who should have been her friends, who still had nothing to say to her after the debacle of her near-graduation, and wondered what the hell was going on.

When Cora's group reached their assigned classroom, the matron waiting for them was one of the ones who had been responsible for Cora during her recent stay in solitary. Cora offered her the politest, blandest of smiles and sat at the front of the room, folding her hands atop the desk and looking attentively to the chalkboard, where a series of equations had been written for them to study.

"Are you well, Miss Miller?" asked the matron.

"Yes, ma'am," said Cora. "May I answer problem two?"

The matron allowed that she could.

The class progressed according to the structure of such things, with questions being asked and answers being offered. None of the girls acted up, not even Sumi, who kept her head down and participated without causing a disruption, treating the math with the seriousness it deserved. History progressed in much the same way, as did biology.

Midway through the group's grammar lesson, the door opened and the headmaster stepped inside. All conversation immediately stopped. Even the matron looked startled by his presence, lowering the pointer she'd been using to indicate verb conjugations on the chalkboard.

"Pardon the intrusion," he said, a smile on his pleasant, forgettable face. "I'm here to borrow Miss Miller, if you don't mind."

"Of course not, Headmaster," said the matron. "Miss Miller?"

But Cora was already standing, crisp and quiet and mannerly, looking at the headmaster with the vague air of someone who was sure something interesting was about to happen, and was prepared to pay proper attention to it. She walked to his side without a word, and didn't flinch or pull away when he settled his hand on her shoulder.

Only Emily, whose seat was at a slight angle compared to the rest of the room, noticed the way Cora's fingers twitched, like they wanted to form fists, like they wanted to be ready to swing. She continued looking blandly forward, not betraying what she knew. This plan, haphazard and dangerous as it was, depended on every one of them playing their part. Even Rowena, who put her hand up as soon as Cora stood, waiting to be acknowledged.

"Yes, Miss Crest?" said the matron, after a moment had passed without Rowena rethinking her actions.

Rowena lowered her hand. "Will we be giving Cora time to return before we finish today's lesson? She's been absent from class for the better part of the week, and I'd prefer not to spend more of my leisure time than necessary helping her catch up. I have essays to write for my other classes."

"A reasonable question," said the headmaster, hand still resting on Cora's shoulder. "Miss Lennox, you have permission to take your class on a nature walk. Something brisk and educational. I'll have Miss Miller back by the time you return."

It took most of the class a moment to realize that "Miss Lennox" was the matron. She had been teaching them periodically for months, slipping in and out of the classroom according to whatever private schedule controlled the school staff, and none of them had ever heard her name before. The matron herself looked faintly alarmed, glancing at the headmaster. He didn't appear to notice. His attention was back on the silently, patiently waiting Cora.

"Shall we go, Miss Miller?" he asked.

Cora tilted her head, offering him a pleasant, perfectly bland smile that was rendered somehow complicated by the way her rainbow-painted hair framed her face. She looked like she was becoming someone else.

"Of course, Headmaster," she said, and her voice was hers and wasn't hers at the same time, steady and calm and serene.

The headmaster nodded one more time to the matron—to *Miss Lennox,* and knowing her name was a kind of heady, breathtaking power that most of the students hadn't tasted in so, so long—before he turned, pulling Cora along with him, and stepped out of the room.

The hall was empty, as it always was when classes were in session, and their footsteps echoed ahead of them, like tiny sonic bursts mapping their environment. Cora kept her eyes forward, not looking at anything in particular, allowing herself to be led. The headmaster was less sanguine. He kept stealing glances at her, like he wasn't sure what he was seeing, like he wanted to somehow change it. Like he thought he knew how.

When they reached his office, he led her inside, gestured her toward a seat, and moved to settle in his own chair, behind his sturdy oak desk. It was an imposing thing, that chair, all black leather and polished metal. It was a chair for a powerful person, for someone who made important decisions for everyone around them. It was a chair for a headmaster.

Cora was unable to fully control the small curl of her lip when she looked at it. It was a chair that would have looked lovely at the center of a bonfire. It would probably smell like bacon when it burned, and the castors in the wheels would pop and shimmer in the firelight. Cora's expression smoothed back into pleasant neutrality at the thought. Everything could burn, if she was willing to put the effort in.

"It's good to see you doing so well," said the headmaster, studying Cora as he sat. If he'd seen the brief wrinkle in her serenity, he didn't say anything. "I admit, I was concerned about you after your most recent readjustment. There was some question of whether we'd been moving too quickly with you."

"I've realized that you can only help me so far before I have to help myself," said Cora. She held up one hand, showing its complete lack of rainbows. "I've faced down some of my demons at last, and I'll be ready to rejoin the world outside very soon."

"You'll forgive me if I'm not as eager to believe that as some of the matrons."

"You've seen many students come and go," said Cora. "You have reason to be suspicious when a problem child turns themselves around too quickly. I understand why you're not going to be immediately convinced of my motivations."

"You say all the right things," said the headmaster. "It's odd, for a traveler to give up on their door so quickly. Many of our students stay here until they age out of the program, and return home unsuited for normal society. Their parents are very disappointed in them."

"My parents have always supported me," said Cora neutrally.

"Your admission papers say that they thought you had committed suicide when you first disappeared. Do you have much experience with death, Miss Miller?"

Cora looked at him levelly. "More than I would like." Sailors whose ships had sailed into the wrong waters, gasping out their last breath in her arms. The deep cold waters of the Moors, where the Drowned Gods had seized her fast and pulled her down, down into the depths, the unforgiving depths, where nothing was forgotten or forgiven.

The sailors had been heroes in their own stories, and the mermaids had been the monsters. But it didn't matter who wore which label. When monsters met heroes, there were always casualties.

The headmaster might have been a hero, once. He was a monster now. There was going to be a casualty, even if he didn't kill bodies. The only question left was which one of them was walking away.

"I'll be frank, Miss Miller: I think you're trying to trick me. I think your little friend from Miss West's school came on some sort of ill-conceived rescue mission, and you think you're going to walk away. I would like to state, in so many words, that it's not going to happen. You *will* remain here until you turn eighteen, and at that point, you can choose to drop out, or you can choose to do the sensible thing for your own future, or you can choose to leave. I think you'll find that it won't matter if this was a trick: the door you so eagerly seek will be closed to you."

"I understand," said Cora. "I assure you, this isn't a trick. I was right to come here. The rainbows are gone from my skin. My hair will change next, I'm sure, and I'll be saved. It's nice to play sometimes. But you can't live your whole life running toward rainbows. Rainbows won't feed you or clothe you or put a roof over your head. All they'll do is shine. Lots of things can shine. I think I'd like to shine. I'll just do it quietly."

There was a pause as the headmaster looked at her and Cora did her best to keep breathing, to keep looking at him with calm, untroubled eyes. This was another kind of war. This was a battle, and she knew how to win battles. All too often, the trick was in refusing to be the first one to move.

Finally, the headmaster nodded. "I don't entirely believe you yet," he said.

"I can't blame you for that."

"But if, as you say, you're willing to change your behavior, I would be delighted to welcome you back to the fellowship of humanity." The headmaster smiled. It wasn't the terrible smile he'd shown her during her intake, all teeth and ill intent, but it wasn't a kind smile, either, and it only made the slightest of impression on his general air of forgettable blandness.

Cora took a careful breath. This was a gamble, and one that might have been better left for another time . . . but gambles were risky by nature, and if this one paid off, it might make her position substantially better. That made it worth trying.

"Sir, may I ask a question?"

"Yes, Miss Miller?"

"I can't . . . I know you when I see you, but I can't remember your face when I'm not looking directly at it. Why is that?"

And the headmaster's smile widened.

12 THE HEADMASTER'S TALE

"THE DOORS HAVE ALWAYS been more inclined to prey on little girls," said the headmaster, and Cora said nothing. He was a man who enjoyed being listened to: anyone with eyes could see that. He liked it when people made him feel important, and attention had always been a quick route to importance. Attention said "you exist." Attention said "I see you."

She supposed that for a man who disappeared from the mind's eye as soon as he was out of sight, being seen might be even more important than it was for most people.

"That doesn't mean boy children are safe, only that they're less likely to see the lures, or to recognize them as the signs they are. Their parents prepare them for other dangers, other risks. They keep them safe from strangers and from busy highways. They don't keep them safe from impossible doors."

Cora found her silence was too heavy to hold. She had to put it down. "My parents never warned me about the doors, sir."

"They told you to be quiet and constrained and obedient, didn't they? That's virtually the same thing. The doors want wild things. They want feral beasts in the skin of dutiful daughters—and you can't sit here, with your neatly brushed hair and your tidy uniform and tell me you don't know what it is to be feral. I know you too well for that."

Cora said nothing.

"I was a good boy. I listened to my elders, I did my lessons,

I tried to behave. And one day, there was a door where no door belonged, and I opened it, and found myself in a world where color was a fairy tale. It was a cut-paper reality, black and white and malleable, and I was a god there, because I understood how to move in three dimensions. I taught the people so many things they thought were impossible because the rules of possibility were different for them. I made their world infinitely better, and when I was done, they asked if I would stay. They offered me the paper moon and the cardboard stars if I would be their new leader. I could have ushered them into a golden age. But I missed my family. I missed food with shape and texture, that didn't feel like sawdust in my mouth, no matter how glorious it tasted. I was born for this world, Miss Miller, even as you were, and I wanted—I *needed*—to return to it. The doors tell their children to be sure. Well, I was sure I needed to go. I told them so. I told them I had done all that I could. And do you know how they replied?"

Cora shook her head, still silent. This time, her silence was not by choice. It was the swallowed horror of someone who could see the shape of the story coming together in front of them, and wished, very much, that they had the power to look away.

"They said I couldn't go without allowing them to give me a gift, because I had been so very good to them, and so kind, and they couldn't stand the thought of me leaving empty-handed. And then they held me down, all my smiling, friendly companions, the people who I'd come to care for almost as family, and they stripped the individuality from my bones, so no one in *this* world would be able to remember me between one moment and the next. My parents, when I came staggering into the backyard, had almost forgotten they had ever had a son. My sister had moved into my bedroom. I could remind them I was real, when I made an effort, but I would simply . . . slip out of their minds every time I turned my back.

"It got better as I grew older, as the magic faded. Not enough—never enough—but people started to remember my name. The internet was a blessing. No one needed to know what my face looked like if they only spoke to me in text. I focused on my studies, got good grades, and decided to do everything in my power to help other children who found themselves in the position I had been in. I had to save them, you see, as no one had come to save me. I had to save *you,* Miss Miller. It's not too late for you to be saved."

Solemnly, Cora nodded. "I appreciate your efforts."

The headmaster blinked, looking somewhat taken aback. It was clear he had expected her to argue with him, or at least to put up more of a resistance. "Good," he said. "Now it's time for us to test your new resolve."

"Sir?"

"Your class will be on the grounds, enjoying their nature walk. I want you to go find them." The headmaster smiled his terrible smile again, seeming to have his equilibrium back. "There are trees outside. There's a lake elsewhere on the grounds, gloriously deep and inviting. I want to see if you can ignore those things to make the responsible choice. I want to see if you're serious."

"Thank you, sir." Cora stood. "I won't let you down."

"Then you will be very surprising indeed," said the headmaster.

Cora left the room as fast as she dared. Rushing might send the wrong impression, might make him think she was in a hurry to be away from him—which she was, of course she was, but she didn't want *him* to think that. She wanted him to think they were the very best of friends now, or at least that she understood and respected his position.

It was good to know that he'd been through a door himself, and better to know what kind of world he'd gone to visit. There was no way he could hear how fast her heart was beating, or smell the mixture of terror and elation rising off her skin. His world had been organized and fixated on rules and rewards, and that explained a few things, too, because Virtuous travelers could never understand that Wicked children weren't entirely built of spite and breaking the rules, that they could be obedient, or wild, or anything else a Virtuous child could be. As long as she seemed to be following the rules without complaint, he wouldn't see the Wickedness in her. And as long as she remembered why she was doing this, she wouldn't lose track of it herself.

The hall was still empty. Cora walked with quick, efficient steps to the nearest approved exit, nodding politely to the matron there, who made no move to stop her. That was another advantage of this school's narrow way of looking at its students. Everyone knew she was Wicked-forged. While she was behaving like she wasn't herself anymore, she was doing what they wanted. She could be forgiven.

The air outside was like a slap to the back of her throat, so sweet it hurt. Cora sucked in a greedy breath, holding it as she walked, so that it became a pleasant burn when she finally breathed out again. Walk, inhale, walk, exhale. The sky was gray, studded with clouds, beautiful in its own way. She kept walking, heading for the line of the trees, where the nature appreciation trails would unspool themselves.

Nature appreciation was a key component of the Whitethorn method. By teaching students to appreciate the world they had, they could convince those same students to loosen their grasp on the world they were supposed to be forgetting. Cora liked nature appreciation. It was all lectures and hands-off, no-touching, but at least it was outside, in the open air. She'd take outside even without the lake any day.

Some of the girls weren't even allowed that much. They were the ones who'd gone to worlds with too much nature and not enough civilization, the ones who looked at the walls of the school like they were some sort of affront and needed to be torn down. When the rest of the class went on a nature walk, those girls sat inside and read from a pile of carefully selected books and magazines, all touting the wonders of human innovation and the spread of human technology.

Regan was normally part of that group, kept away from anything that might make her think too much about the talking horses and endless farmlands of her home. It was a shock, then, when Cora stepped around a curve in the nature path and nearly slammed right into her.

She was standing right in the middle of the walkway; head tilted back she could see the spreading green branches struggling to block the watery gray sky, and there were tears in her eyes, like this was the most beautiful, impossible thing she'd ever seen.

It was a trap. A trap and a trick and Cora noted its nature even as she felt vaguely insulted that they'd thought she might fall for it. The Serpent had had far more respect for her as an adversary, and the Serpent had *hated* her. These people. They ran a school filled with heroes, and somehow they still thought they could treat them like children and get what they wanted without ever really trying.

They were too far from the school for anyone to be listening in, unless Regan was being more closely escorted than she seemed. Cora stopped, falling back into her polite, polished pose, and tried to pretend to be enthralled by a particularly fascinating bit of lichen. It was purple, ruffled like a lace cuff, and remarkable only because it happened to be positioned so that looking at it offered her an excellent view of the athletic field. There were no matrons hiding in the tangle of the wood, of that much she was sure; they lacked the grace to work their way that deeply into the brush without breaking a trail, and once a trail was broken, students would try to take it, driven by their unkillable need to see more than they were technically allowed.

There was no one. She and Regan were alone. Well, really, she was with Regan, and Regan was alone, still so focused on the trees that she hadn't noticed Cora at all.

"That's a good way to wind up dead, where I come from," said Cora. Regan jumped. Cora paid her no mind. "Ambushes are way easier when the people you're trying to ambush aren't paying any attention to the avenues of attack. You're a trap, you know."

"I thought that might be why they let me outside, but I didn't care if it meant I got to smell the green things, and I still don't care," said Regan. Her voice was worn out, resigned, like she had considered every way this conversation could play out, and decided none of them were worth fighting for. "I guess they know I'm not going to graduate, and they don't want to send me home still broken. So they might as well dangle me for someone like you, to see whether you'll take the bait."

It took Cora a moment to understand what Regan was implying. She scowled, too offended to measure the expression against the sort of things that were considered appropriate and acceptable for a girl like the one she was pretending to be. "So they sent you out here, and you went anyway, even though you thought they were going to have someone come along to *kill* you?"

"You let your friend hit me the last time we talked." There

was a flicker of humor in Regan's eyes. Under all the weariness, she wasn't broken yet.

"Yes, yes, to cover for you so you didn't get in trouble for talking to us," said Cora. "I'm not that kind of killer."

"Don't you mean 'I'm not a killer'?"

"I say what I mean, usually," said Cora. "I'm a killer. I'd bet most of us are, here. Doesn't matter whether you admit it or not. Once you've killed, you're a killer. The difference between a person they write songs about and a person they tell their children to avoid is volume, and how many lungs you ripped out." Cora visibly caught herself, wincing. "Sorry. That was a little . . . intense. I'm not going to hurt you. Actually, I'm glad you're the honeytrap they set for me. I have a question for you."

Regan looked dubious. "What question?"

"You can talk to horses, and to things that *look* like horses but can't possibly be horses. Some of the things you mentioned have feathers. Horses don't have feathers. So is it a shape thing, or a hooves thing, or what? Can you talk to cows? Can you talk to deer?"

"I don't know what it is," said Regan slowly. "I suppose it's more shape than anything else. If something says 'horse' to the part of my brain that knows how to translate, I can do it. I understand what cows are saying, but I don't know how to talk back to them, and I try not to listen too hard. Cows write really bad poetry about grass and clouds and the farmers they see by the fences, and it makes me sad."

"Are you a vegetarian?"

"No, and that's part of why it makes me sad." Regan shrugged. "I like meat. I like sustainable farming practices and ethical slaughter and making the lives of domestic animals as pleasant and stress-free as possible, but I also like hamburgers, and

steaks, and the sort of long-lasting energy I only get from pro-
tein. Honestly, I'm glad I'm not a vegetarian."

"Why?"

"If I was, it would be because I know that cows write poetry. Which would make it part of what I'm supposed to be
learning to forget, and means I would have been living entirely on bacon and bad dreams since I got here. They already
restrict me to an all-meat diet." Regan sighed. "Sometimes I
dream about finding out which of the matrons sets the menu,
and making *her* eat the slop they tell us is food."

"Oh." Cora frowned. "You didn't answer the whole question. What about deer? Can you talk to deer?"

"They look enough like perytons that I can," said Regan.
"Why?"

"Because I don't think any of us has ever *met* the headmaster," said Cora. "We've met a man who *says* he's Headmaster
Whitethorn, and he does a pretty good job, but he's not the
headmaster, and I think we're in an awful lot of danger here, if
we stay."

Regan stared at her. Cora beamed, looking relieved to no
longer be carrying this terrible revelation entirely on her own.

"All right," she said. "Let's go find the rest of my class. If
we're going to start planning a way to get out of here, I guess
we'll need to make sure they can accept you as one of their
own. While we walk, you can tell me about lichen."

"Why lichen?" asked Regan bluntly.

"Because I expect the matron to ask what I was looking at
that took me so long, and lichen's about the most boring thing
I can think of that still might be believable, and you look like
the kind of girl who might know stuff about lichen." Cora
started walking, slow and decorous, leaving Regan plenty of
time to catch up.

"What's that supposed to mean?" asked Regan.

"You can talk to horses. You don't get to question me."

"I like lichen. There's nothing wrong with liking lichen."

"That was exactly my point," said Cora, and laughed, bright as a summer morning, and led her new friend deeper into the woods, away from the looming shape of the school, toward the trembling and uncertain future.

PART IV

JAILBREAK

13 LICHEN AND LIES

CORA'S CLASS WAS CONSIDERABLY deeper into the woods, clustered on the path and studying a leopard-spotted slug with the sort of intensity that most of them normally reserved for more fascinating things. Sumi had found a twig somewhere, and was poking the poor thing in the side. The matron—Miss Lennox, a matron with a *name,* a matron who could be picked out of the herd with an identifying mark, something that branded her as an individual—was standing a short distance away, technically supervising them, but shifting from foot to foot like she no longer quite knew what to do with herself.

That was interesting. Everything about this day had been interesting. Sometimes going undercover among the enemy was the best way to make a bad situation into a slightly better one. Cora approached Miss Lennox, Regan beside her and a pleasantly bland smile on her face.

"I found Miss Lewis in the woods," said Cora. "I think she got lost, because there wasn't anyone with her, but she didn't hide or try to run away when I said hello, which means she can't have been doing anything wrong on purpose. Can we help her find her way back to her dorm?"

Miss Lennox looked briefly confused. "I . . . Miss Lewis, where is your class? Who has responsibility for you right now?"

"I came so close to graduation, and the other Compulsion students don't want to have me around, because they're afraid

I might hold them back." Regan's cheeks burned red with embarrassment. The color deepened as the other students turned to look at her, their eyes bright with the many unexpected excitements of the day.

"I see," said Miss Lennox. "That's—" She stopped, appearing to struggle with whatever she was going to say next.

Cora narrowed her eyes. That was interesting. She'd never seen a matron at a true loss for words before. But Miss Lennox didn't *look* like a matron anymore, did she? She had when the day started, all bland disapproval and interchangeable strictness, but that had been before she had a name. Giving a person a name changed them.

He made a mistake, she thought, and it was a thrill and a delight and so big that she almost missed it when Miss Lennox started talking again.

"Well, that's simply not fair, and not reasonable in the slightest," she said. "Whoever is supposed to be responsible for you should be ashamed of themselves. I know you're not a part of my dorm, but you're welcome to do your studies with us until this can be settled."

Regan's eyes widened. "Do you mean that, ma'am?"

Miss Lennox didn't even look annoyed at being questioned. "Of course I do," she said. "We have a responsibility to make sure you're given a proper education, and part of a proper education is seeing to your social needs and emotional health. I—" She stopped, making a small, startled sound and raising one hand to her forehead, closing her eyes in what was clearly pain.

"Are you all right, ma'am?" asked Sumi, dropping her twig.

"Of course I am." Miss Lennox lowered her hand, the pained expression fading. "My health is not your concern."

Interesting. Following her instincts—which had always

served her well, or at least always been enough to get her out of trouble, even if they were the reason she got *into* trouble a lot of the time—Sumi smiled blandly and said, "Of course not, Miss Lennox. I understand my place. I simply didn't want to disrupt the nature walk with a medical emergency."

Miss Lennox blinked, expression a mixture of confusion and bewilderment, like nothing made sense anymore. It was fascinating. None of them had ever seen a matron look like that before.

"Right," said Miss Lennox. Even her voice was different, dazed and slightly distant. Behind her, the girl without a name looked actively stricken. "Nature walk. Regan, please join us. We're going to look for native flora and record it in our sighting books."

"I would love to," said Regan.

Miss Lennox began walking. The others followed, Regan among them, while Cora hung back, waiting for her chance. When the nameless girl began to walk, Cora reached out and grabbed her elbow, pulling her to a halt. The nameless girl gave her a startled look.

"What are you doing?" she asked.

"We need to talk," said Cora, keeping her voice low to avoid attracting attention. "Will you walk with me?"

"Why should I?" The nameless girl shook free, taking a step to the side to put herself out of reach. "I said I'd help you with this stupid plan of yours, but I'm not taking any risks I don't have to. I'm getting out of here, not getting locked up for painting a target on myself."

"I think I know why you still don't have a name."

The nameless girl stopped breathing.

"The matrons don't have names. The matrons *never* have names. I've seen them go to ridiculous lengths to keep from using anything that might even be shaped like a name—but Miss Lennox has a name now, and it's changing her. Can't you see how it's changing her? Names have power. Names *define* things."

"Why are you being so mean to me?" There were tears in the nameless girl's eyes. "I said I'd help you get out of here. I said I'd go with you. I know I was mean to you before, but this is . . . this is worse than anything I did."

"No." Cora shook her head. "I'm not being mean, I'm telling you to look, and *see*. She didn't have a name and she was happy to be just another matron, all rules and regulations and making sure we toed the line. Now she *does* have a name, and suddenly she knows we're people. I think the headmaster, whoever he is, takes their names away to make sure they do what he wants them to do. I think your name would have come back to you already, if you hadn't been here. If you hadn't been in a place where stolen things are forced to stay stolen."

The nameless girl still looked confused and hurt. None of this was reaching her; it was slamming up against the shields she used to protect herself from an uncaring world. Cora supposed she couldn't blame her, but it was all so *inconvenient*. Things had been easier in the Trenches, when she'd been the only hero around, when everyone had listened to her without thinking twice about whether that was the right thing to do.

To be fair, it hadn't always been. But they'd had an awful lot of fun finding that out.

"How did you lose your name?"

"The . . . the Rat King stole it when I said I didn't want to be his bride," said the nameless girl, voice gone small with pain and memory. "I had to come back here so he couldn't use it against me. My . . . Bright said she thought it would follow me through the door, that the Rat King couldn't hold it if I wasn't there, and then once I had time to recover I could come home, and we could be happy. But I kept getting smaller, and my name didn't follow me. One day I'm going to wake up and I'll be something else. I won't be me anymore. And I won't even be able to go to the Rat King for protection, because he doesn't exist here."

"I'm so sorry that happened to you," said Cora. "But I don't think you're listening to me. I think your name is *here*. It's flittering around the edges of the school grounds, trying to get back to you, and it can't, because it's being stopped by the same magic that keeps the matrons from having names."

"Then why didn't it come back to me as soon as I left?" said the girl, clearly wanting to believe and afraid of false hope. "Why didn't it come back to me all that time before I came here?"

Cora shrugged. "Maybe the curse needed time to wear off," she said. "I bet it would have, if you hadn't come here." She smiled, quick and tight and unamused. "You came here because you thought this was the best place for you. I think it's the *worst* place for you. It's like being allergic to salt and hiding in a seaside cave."

"No one's allergic to salt," said the nameless girl.

"Shows what *you* know." Cora grabbed the nameless girl's elbow again, pulling her along as she followed the group. "The matrons aren't supposed to have names. It makes them into individuals. I don't think the fake headmaster was supposed to say what he did, and someone's going to have to come and steal her name again. If they don't, who knows what might happen? Something wonderful, and they don't want that, not here. Not now."

The nameless girl stumbled as Cora kept pulling her along. "What does all this even *mean*? How is it supposed to help me?"

"Easy. If we take you away from here, I'm betting your

name will find you fast as a hungry shark, because it wants to be with you as much as you want to have it. But getting away means understanding what's going on, and you're small and quiet and fast. Smaller and quieter than Sumi, even, which is a neat trick. So tonight you're going to sneak out, and you're going to watch to see how they take Miss Lennox's name away."

The nameless girl stared at Cora. "You're insane."

"Probably," said Cora placidly. "Sticks and stones, as the sages say; sticks and stones. I know what I am and I'm happy this way, and saying something true shouldn't be an insult, ever, because that's not how words want to work. Don't you want to leave this place? Don't you want to go back where your name can find you, whatever it's shaped like?"

"I already said I wanted to go," said the nameless girl.

"Good." Cora bared her teeth in a smile. "Now act like it."

The group had stopped to study a small, flowering bush gamely struggling to hold on despite the encroaching chill of fall. Cora made silent note of the perplexed expression on Miss Lennox's face, like all of this was somehow new to her, like she had never seen this trail, or these students, or a flowering bush before in her life.

Whatever the false headmaster had done when he so casually gave the matron back her name, it was waking her up, bringing her rapidly through levels of self-awareness that she might not even have realized she had been losing. Cora narrowed her eyes, watching the woman move. She was jerky, unsteady, like a fawn finding its legs. She was lost.

She had been lost.

Slowly, like she was approaching a wild and wounded animal, Cora skirted the group to stand beside Miss Lennox. "There's something I've always wondered, ma'am. Is it appropriate for me to ask you a question?"

"Of course," said Miss Lennox, sounding distracted, like everything around her was simply too much, like it had to be absorbed one slow beat at a time. "I'm your teacher. You have to ask me questions if you're going to learn."

"When did you graduate?"

"I didn't," said Miss Lennox automatically. Then she froze, the animation draining from her face until she looked like a statue of flesh and bone. The girls all turned to look at her, sensing, in the way of bored teens, that something interesting was about to happen.

Miss Lennox clutched the sides of her head and began screaming.

It was a high, shrill sound, like the wail of an animal with its leg caught in a trap, or the screaming of a child who'd just realized they were somehow horribly, inexplicably alone in the world. Miss Lennox dropped to her knees, still screaming. Rowena stumbled backward. Stephanie moved more smoothly. Emily seemed to root in place, becoming an unobtrusive part of the environment. Even Regan and the nameless girl moved, putting distance between themselves and something they instinctively recognized as dangerous.

Only Sumi moved toward the sound. She put a hand on Miss Lennox's shoulder, bearing down slightly, so that her presence would have both weight and immediacy.

"It's all coming back to you, isn't it?" she asked, glancing to Cora as she spoke. Many people would have been surprised by the gentleness in her voice, the understanding; she sounded like a general trying to talk a foot soldier back from the edge. The scattered, sometimes incomprehensible girl was gone, replaced by someone who had seen too much, and would never be able to forget it.

Many people would have been surprised, but almost as

many wouldn't have been. They knew what it was to bury yourself in dreams to escape from the nightmares. They knew what it meant to survive.

"If you didn't graduate, then you weren't willing to let go," Sumi continued. She began stroking Miss Lennox's hair with one hand. "There was something waiting on the other side of the door, and all you could think about was finding a way back there, back to *them*. Friends or lovers or family, it doesn't matter, because they took your name and they didn't let you go home, and now you're here and everything is strange and it hurts. I know. I'm sorry."

Miss Lennox kept screaming.

Sumi had trouble guessing the age of adults sometimes: they got mad when you guessed too high, and sometimes they laughed when you guessed too young. Still, she could tell Miss Lennox wasn't a teenager, and probably hadn't been for quite some time. She was probably somewhere in her late twenties or early thirties. More than a decade from her graduation date. More than a decade from home.

Footsteps pounded along the path. Sumi turned to see three more matrons running toward them, cheeks flushed and eyes bright with panic. A decision had to be made. Sumi stepped forward, projecting innocence just as hard as she possibly could.

"We were looking at that plant over there"—she pointed to the flowering bush—"and she started screaming. I think maybe something bit her? I don't know. Can you help us?" She took a hiccupping breath, allowing her eyes to fill with frightened tears. It was easy to pull her fear forward, to wrap it around herself like a blanket. If this didn't work, if they didn't get away . . .

Cora moved to stand next to Sumi, a reassuring wall of girl, offering comfort through her presence alone.

The matrons slowed to a stop, looking from the still-screaming Miss Lennox to Sumi, and finally to the other students, who weren't faking their confusion or dismay. Regan looked like she was on the verge of hyperventilating. The nameless girl was half-hiding behind Stephanie, eyes filled with vivid terror.

"None of you said or did *anything* to trigger this response?" asked one of the matrons. She pointed to Regan. "*She* isn't part of your class."

"She doesn't have a class, ma'am," said Cora. "She didn't graduate, and now the other girls from her dorm don't want her around. Our matron said she could come on the nature walk, so her education wouldn't be underserved."

It was clear from the looks on the matrons' faces that they didn't believe her. It was equally clear that something had to give. Miss Lennox was starting to whine between screams, a high, agonized sound that made the hairs on the back of Cora's neck stand on end. Nothing healthy should make a sound like that one. Nothing *sane*.

"Fine," said the tallest matron, voice tight. "All of you, return to your dorm at once. We will send someone to fetch you for supper." She turned her attention to Miss Lennox. Just like that, they were dismissed.

"Come on." Cora grabbed Regan by the hand and began dragging her along the path, away from the matrons, away from Miss Lennox. She felt a pang of regret at that. She would have liked to save her. "All of you, quick."

"Where are we going?" asked Regan. The rest of the girls followed, so schooled in the ways of quick obedience that it was clear they hadn't considered doing anything else.

"Different places. Come *on*." Cora kept walking until they reached the end of the path, where it widened out onto the grassy field, ending at the terrible structure of the school. She let go of Regan's hand, took a breath, and turned to face the others.

"I'm leaving," she said. "I'm leaving, and I'm taking Sumi with me, and we're not looking back. Rowena, I know you want to stay here. That's your choice. I need to know whether you can be quiet and let the rest of us go."

Rowena looked from Cora to the others, her normal arrogance melting into uncertainty. "I haven't told on you yet."

"We haven't *done* anything yet. We've talked about doing, and we've talked about being unhappy, but we haven't *done*. Now is where we start doing. If you can't let us do, you need to say, so I can put you out of the way."

Fear sparked in Rowena's eyes. "You mean kill me?"

"I mean put you out of the way. I don't think this will take long enough for you to really be hurt. I think it's all going to happen very quickly now." Cora looked at her levelly. "I don't kill innocent people. That's not what a hero does. But I don't stand back and let people endanger my friends. That's not what a hero does, either. You can't say 'my hands are clean, that means I'm a good guy' when you let people stand behind you with knives, ready to slash at everyone you say you want to save."

Rowena held her breath. So did Stephanie, and the nameless girl. Regan, Emily, and Sumi said nothing at all. Finally, Rowena looked away.

"I'll be quiet," she spat. "I want to stay here, but that doesn't mean I want to hurt—" Her mouth worked soundlessly, unable to find a name to fix on, until she gestured angrily to the nameless girl. "—my friend. I don't want to hurt my friend. The rest of you can go screw yourselves."

"Thank you," whispered the nameless girl.

Cora only nodded. "Okay. Regan."

"Yes?"

"No one's keeping track of you right now. That's a good thing. I want you to go into the woods, as far as you can, and find a deer. Ask them to show you how to get out of here."

"She can talk to deer," said Emily. "Of course she can talk to deer. Nothing else makes sense about today, so why shouldn't she be able to talk to deer?"

"What am I supposed to do if I find them?" asked Regan.

"Wait in the woods." Cora managed a smile. It wasn't a very encouraging one. "We'll be out by moonrise."

Then she turned and walked toward the building. The others followed, and Regan was left outside, alone.

14 THE POWER OF NAMES

EMILY MANAGED TO HOLD her tongue until they were back in their dorm with the door closed. As soon as they were safe, she rounded on Cora, demanding, "What's your plan? How are we getting out of here?"

"Tell me about your door," said Cora.

Emily blinked. "It was . . . I found it in one of those janky haunted houses people set up around Halloween," she said. "It was next to the exit. It said 'be sure' on it in these dripping blood letters, so I figured it was the way to get to a bigger scare. Instead, it led to a world where it was always harvest, where it was Halloween every night, and I danced with monsters and sang with scarecrows, and I was happy."

"Uh-huh," said Cora. She turned to Stephanie. "You?"

"Dinosaurs," she said. Her tone turned beatific. "I went where there were dinosaurs."

"Right." Cora turned to the nameless girl. "You?"

"I already told you."

"You told me how it ended. How did it *begin*?"

The nameless girl took a breath. "There was a door in the foundation of our house. I'd been . . . My father had been drinking, he'd been hitting my mom, all I wanted was to get away. So I got away."

"Yeah." Cora turned to Rowena. "You?"

"I'm not part of your little gang," said Rowena. "I'm here because I want to be."

"That isn't—"

"I'm *eleven*." Rowena spat the words out like they tasted sour. "Okay? I'm eleven. I was missing for three hours, and when I found my way back through the veil of clocks to the door, I looked like I was six years older than I was supposed to be. I fell through the door when I was six and I came back out physically twelve. My parents don't believe I am who I say I am. I've been here for five years and I could graduate tomorrow, if I had anywhere to go. You can all go running back to your happy little fantasy worlds. If *I* went back through my door, I'd be dead of old age in less than a month. So leave me out of this."

Cora nodded. "You're making the right choice," she said. She paused. "The veil of clocks . . . can you do anything with time?"

"What? No."

"It was worth asking." She turned back to the others. "Now that we all know what we're watching for, we leave tonight. I honestly expect at least one of those doors to show up as soon as we're clear of the grounds."

"How?" asked Stephanie. "The doors are locked, the grounds are walled, and the matrons are everywhere."

"The false headmaster gave us the key, even if he didn't mean to," said Cora. "When he gave Miss Lennox back her name, he broke whatever hold this place has over its graduates. He brought her back to herself. The matrons will be distracted, trying to help her."

"Why do you call him the false headmaster?" asked Emily.

"No one remembers him when they're not looking at him," said Cora. "He can't *build* anything. He's a nasty man, full of nasty thoughts, and most of them are about being forgotten. I think that's why he gave Miss Lennox her name back. To punish her for what we did. He wanted her to remember, even if it was only for a little while, that she was going to be forgotten. His door . . . wasn't kind to him."

None of the doors were *kind,* not really, not even when they gave people exactly what they wanted. The Trenches hadn't been *kind* to her. They had given her the freedom to figure out who she was. But they had also given her a war, and a hundred drowned sailors, and the smell of blood mixed with saltwater. They had given her nightmares that would be with her until the day she died. They had given her scars, and only some of them were visible.

"So?" Rowena folded her arms. "Being headmaster doesn't make you a nice person."

"What's the name of the school?"

"The Whitethorn Institute. Don't be stupid."

"If the man we've met is the headmaster, and he's completely forgettable, how do we know the name of the school? If it's his name, too, we should forget it. It hasn't been stolen from *him,* but the things he went through on the other side of his door stole it from everybody else." Cora spread her hands. "We haven't met the headmaster. We're being lied to. We're being lied to and held captive and I'm done. We leave tonight."

"How?" asked Emily.

Sumi grinned, seizing the dialog. "Nonsensically." She turned to the nameless girl. "You're good at fitting in little places. Go find a way into the matrons' quarters. See what happens when they take Miss Lennox's name away from her. See where they *put* it. And then come back here, and we'll smash everything we have to smash, and we'll go find Regan and her deer, and they'll lead us out of here."

"Are you sure?" asked the nameless girl timidly.

"No," said Cora. "But it's the only chance we've got."

15 TWO SIDES OF THE STORY

REGAN WALKED THROUGH THE forest as if it were the most familiar, beloved place in the world; as if she knew every inch of it, and every inch of it knew her. The creatures of the wood reacted in kind. They didn't flee at the sound of her footsteps, but inched closer, moving through the brush to watch her as she came. One particularly bold blue jay dropped so low that his wings brushed her hair as he flew by, and her laughter was all the brighter because she hadn't laughed in so very, terribly long.

She had always been a solemn child, slow to make friends, slow to trust anyone's intentions. She'd had her reasons—of course she'd had her reasons; most adults even agreed that they made sense, even as most children called her stuck-up and arrogant and weird when they thought she wasn't listening, even as the girl she'd trusted most in the world had shared a secret that wasn't hers to share and broken Regan's heart in half—but all the reasons in the world can't change the end result. She'd been lonely, she'd been angry, and when a door had appeared where a door had no business being, she hadn't hesitated.

In a way, she supposed she was one of the lucky ones. She'd come back from her adventures to a family that loved her, even if they couldn't understand who she'd become. That was all right. They hadn't been able to understand her before. They'd loved her and they'd cared for her and they'd blamed themselves for the way she was and they'd blamed her for not mysteriously

becoming different, and when they'd told her that she was going away to boarding school in order to "get over her ordeal,"
she'd packed without complaint, because she'd assumed that
anything had to be better than walking through a house filled
with cool, accusing shadows.

She'd been wrong, of course. Home at least had the horses,
had the trees behind the house, had the kids who'd treated her
like an outsider for most of her life and at least couldn't find
anything new to torment her about. School was an unfamiliar
country, filled with adults who wanted her to deny everything
she knew to be true, and kids who were torn between a deep,
angry denial of their situation and an even deeper, even an-
grier desire to find their doors, to go home. All any of them
wanted was to go home. It was just the shape of the idea that
changed.

Regan stepped into a clearing, her feet as light on the forest floor as the hooves of any wild thing, and stopped in her
tracks at the sight of a single stag cropping at the ground. He
wasn't the sort of deer who gets stories written about him: no
one from the Disney Corporation was going to cast him in
their live-action remake of *Bambi*. One of his antlers was broken. His coat was moth-eaten, mangy, and things moved in it,
a density of fleas and parasites so high that they were visible to
the naked eye. He was favoring his right hind leg over his left,
and when he raised his head to look at her, the insides of his
ears were caked with grime, and the corners of his eyes were
thick with mucus.

He was the most beautiful thing she had seen in so long
that she thought her heart might break from it.

"I don't feel the need to run from you," said the stag. "Why
is that? Humans are a menace."

"I'm halfway yours," said Regan. "The other half of me is

human, and that's useful, because thumbs." She held up her hands and wiggled her thumbs at him in illustration.

"My name is Lord of the Forest," said the stag.

Regan nodded. Every stag she'd ever met had been named Lord of the Forest, even when there was another stag only a few feet away. Deer didn't understand irony. "My name is Regan," she said. "In the name of the Great Alliance of Hooves and Hands, I greet you."

The stag flicked an ear. "That's a name I haven't heard since I was a fawn," he said. "What do you want from me, Regan of the Alliance?"

"The wall around this wood was built to hold human children, not Lords and Ladies of the Forest," she said. "My friends and I need to find a way out." Inwardly, she was rejoicing. *I'm talking to a stag,* she thought, and it was light and lightning in her veins, it was joy beyond comprehension. *It all happened. I was right the whole time. It happened.*

"Why should I help you?"

"Because you know what agony it would be to have your freedom taken away, and you're too good, too gracious, to allow that to happen to anyone else." Regan bowed her head. "Please."

The stag flicked an ear, considering her. Finally, sounding almost bored, he said, "Follow me."

Regan straightened, smiling bright as a prairie sunrise, and let the stag lead her deeper into the wood.

16 SIDES CHOSEN, CHOICES MADE

EVEN AS REGAN WAS remembering what it meant to breathe, the girl who no longer had a name crept along the edge of the hall in the main building of the school, her back bent and her head hunched, willing herself unseen. She knew where the cameras were, thanks to weeks and months of observation, and she knew how to flatten herself out, to fit into their blind spots. It was a necessary skill to possess, especially when living with the daily fear that eventually dwindling would become shrinking would become regressing. The day she was more rat than girl, she would need to be ready to go into hiding, to find a way into the walls in order to save herself from an exterminator's hands. The headmaster—fake, real, it didn't matter—would never tolerate vermin sleeping in a bed like a real person. It didn't matter that she *was* real, that she had always been real. She'd die for the crime of not wanting to love a monster.

Back when she'd been—and even the thought of her name turned to roaring static, making her wince and almost straighten into the path of a camera's lens—*before*, she'd been happy enough, if unchallenged and unfulfilled. She'd walked in a world of low expectations, too pretty to be clever, too clever to be kind, a pig-in-the-middle girl with her future mapped out for her by the adults who smiled indulgently whenever she tried to ask a question. She would graduate from high school, go on to college for a nice, safe degree, something that would make her better equipped to be a good wife one day, a good helper for a man who was a little less attractive and a little more clever, and maybe both those things were a matter of opinion, but that didn't matter. What mattered was that she get good grades, wear the right brands, say the right things, and always, always be on display.

Maybe that was why she'd slipped through a door and into a world where being seen was never the goal, where learning to hide and run and get away were the most important things. She'd found peace on the other side of a doorway that couldn't possibly exist, and when that peace had been stripped away, she'd run away home with a curse hanging over her head and a tongue that no longer remembered what it was to utter her own name.

At first, that had seemed like the only consequence; at first, she'd thought she might be able to find ways around it, to do work that didn't require her to have a name. Maybe her enforced anonymity could even be an asset. She could be some billionaire's secretary, untraceable because she couldn't ever be named, suited to fulfill their every need.

But then she'd started shrinking. Then she'd started finding coarse brown hairs on her pillow in the morning, stiff and unbending, like the guard hairs on a rat's back. Then she'd started waking up in the middle of the night with an aching tailbone, wondering whether this was when the tail was going to worm its way through her flesh, extending indelibly behind her, becoming an immutable part of who she was. She didn't know the full shape of the Rat King's curse, but she had a feeling, too strong to ignore, that once the tail sprouted, it would be too late for her to ever get her name back. Too late for her to ever be human again.

She crept through the school, silent as a sigh, until she reached the science classroom and slipped inside. The cameras in this room were out, had been since a bad accident in chemistry earlier in the week; their gleaming glass eyes saw nothing, transmitted nothing to the school's security office. Carefully, she placed a chair on top of the matron's desk and climbed onto it, straining until her fingertips brushed the paneled ceiling. A shove, a leap, an agonizing pull-up and she was inside, moving through the space between the dropped ceiling and the roof with quick precision. Her back didn't even come close to brushing the actual rafters. Dust tickled her nose and she breathed it in, relaxing into the safe, familiar scent that lingered in enclosed places.

Maybe it wouldn't be so bad, to be a rat. Maybe she could be happy. Or maybe it wouldn't matter. Rats didn't have names the way people did. Maybe they didn't care about happiness the way people did, either.

The school was large, but she'd been there for more than a year, and she knew where she needed to go. Inch by inch, she pulled herself along, until she felt warm air coming up through the small holes in the ceiling tiles. She was nowhere near the student dormitories. Carefully, she stopped, wedged her nails into the space at the edge of the nearest tile, and eased it an inch or so away from its frame, peering downward.

The matrons were gathered in a single central room, sitting in silent contemplation of the air. All save for Miss Lennox, who was moving from body to body, shaking them, grasping their hands, trying to get them to react to her.

"Please, Caroline, please," she moaned, dropping to her knees in front of one matron, a pretty woman about Miss Lennox's age, with freckled cheeks and the empty stare of a mannequin. "We were supposed to get out of here together, remember? You and me and whatever door was willing to have us, forever, no matter what anyone said. Don't you remember?"

The freckle-faced matron stirred slightly, the ghost of a frown tugging at her lips, and then was still. Miss Lennox took her hands.

"I don't know what they did to us, but I know you're in there," she said. "I know you can hear me. It's me, Julia. You can always hear me. Fight, Carrie. Fight, and come back to me."

"That will be quite enough of that."

Miss Lennox gasped and jumped to her feet, moving to put her body between the other matron and the voice. The nameless girl squirmed into a new position in the ceiling, careful to keep her weight off the tiles, and scanned for the voice's owner.

The man in front of the door was familiar: she'd seen him around the school with a mop in his hand and a bucket by his feet, mopping and scrubbing and wiping away the signs that children infested the building, tracking their filth and foolishness everywhere. He was wearing a gray jumpsuit, and had a wide, unremarkable face, easy to overlook, but impossible to forget.

His eyes were sharp as stones. They seemed to see everything. The nameless girl held her breath, lest he should look up and see *her*.

"You," breathed Miss Lennox. "I remember . . . I remember you. You're Headmaster Whitethorn. You didn't want us to know that. You wanted us to think you were the janitor. You . . . you *hurt* me."

"I never intended to, and you have my sincere apologies," said the headmaster. The *real* headmaster. "You failed to graduate. Something had to be done, and I've taken care of you, haven't I? You've had a roof over your head and food in your stomach, which is more than the world outside my walls would have promised you. You've helped my work."

"Your work?" Miss Lennox stared at him. "You stripped

our free will and kept us as prisoners. Carrie doesn't even recognize me!"

"Of course not. She isn't . . . that name you said. She's one of my matrons, interchangeable, serene. Ready to serve. I'll have words with my stand-in. He's supposed to know better than to disrupt the pattern. I'm so sorry. You should never have needed to suffer this way." The headmaster took a step forward. "It'll be over soon."

There was a choice to be made here. Sumi had asked the nameless girl to find out how the names were being taken, where they were being stored—even why the real headmaster was hiding himself. The nameless girl wasn't sure how many of those questions she could answer, but she knew she could get more answers than she had so far. She could learn.

Or she could help.

For a moment—just a moment—she closed her eyes and thought about Bright, the curve of her smile and the cupped shape of her ears, which were closer to a mouse's than a human's, covered in soft fur, like velvet, and so sensitive that she had come apart under the nameless girl's hands every time they held each other. She thought about running through secret tunnels hand in hand, about the taste of mushroom cutlets and glowing caveberries, about feeling like she had a future, not just a frail and fading memory of one.

Bright would understand. If there was ever another traveler, and that child somehow knew the story of the girl who'd lost first her name and then her chance at coming home, Bright would understand.

The nameless girl opened her eyes and shoved the ceiling tile away at the same time. It landed on the floor with a clatter. The headmaster turned to stare at it, then looked up at the hole in the ceiling. He was so focused on it that he didn't notice when another tile moved aside above him. The nameless girl dropped out of the opening, landing on his back and wrapping her arms around his neck, cutting off his oxygen supply.

"Run, Miss Lennox!" she howled. "Run *now*!"

And Miss Lennox, to her credit, did. She grabbed Caroline by the hand and raced for the door, leaving the other matrons behind. The headmaster clawed at the nameless girl's arm, trying to break her grasp. She ground her teeth and held on fast, refusing to be dislodged. Her size helped her. She was stronger than anyone expected her to be, denser than she looked, and her grip was strong: he couldn't get the leverage to throw her off.

"You stole their names," she spat, voice close to his ear, where he couldn't help hearing her. "You kept my name from finding me. I don't know why you're doing this and I don't know who you are, but you're a monster, and I hate you."

The headmaster choked and wheezed. The nameless girl held on tighter. When he finally dropped to his knees, when he finally fell, she kept holding on, until she was absolutely sure that he was unconscious, not just faking. Then—only then— she let go and staggered to her feet, turning to stare at the blank-faced, motionless matrons all around her. None of them seemed to have noticed, or to care, that two of their number had fled; none of them seemed bothered that she had just choked a man to unconsciousness in front of them.

"I'm sorry," she said, and turned and fled, out into the hall, along its silent length and around the school's many corners until she reached the familiarity of her dorm.

The door was open. Miss Lennox and her still blank-eyed

companion were standing in the hall outside; Sumi and Cora were standing in the doorway.

"Please, you have to believe me," said Miss Lennox. "It isn't safe for you here. It isn't safe for *any* of us here. The headmaster—he wants to seal the doors forever. For the sake of the world. He'll never let you leave."

"What about the graduations?" asked Cora.

"Graduates forget," said Miss Lennox. "As soon as they step off of school grounds, they forget, and they think they were sent here because they'd had some sort of breakdown. The ones who won't let go of their doors never graduate." She shuddered. "When I was a student, I wondered what happened to them. I don't have to wonder anymore."

"The headmaster's a wizard," said Cora.

"He's a monster," said Miss Lennox.

"We're not the only students here," said Cora.

Miss Lennox shook her head. "We can come back. We can find people who believe us, other travelers who didn't wind up here, and we can come back, but we *can't* stay, and we *can't* save everyone. Not right now. Not with the resources we have."

"We have a way out of here," said Sumi. "But I don't know if you can take it. You're older than eighteen."

To the nameless girl's surprise, Miss Lennox laughed.

"That's just a number, Sumi: it doesn't mean anything. People say it's when you become an adult, but that isn't universal. You're Japanese American. In Japan, the age of majority is twenty. So when do you get too old to open a door?"

Sumi looked impressed. "How did you—"

"I've heard 'we keep them until the doors lock' more times than I care to count, and I am telling you, age means nothing.

Age is experience, not absolution. If you've found a way to pry open a door, I will go through it, and I will survive whatever's waiting there. We both will. Now please. We have to go."

Sumi smiled.

17 THE LONG ROAD HOME

THEY LEFT THE SCHOOL like thieves fleeing the scene of a crime, quickly, quietly, and with only what they could carry. Sumi left her shoes behind.

They ran, five students and two teachers, across the field behind the institute, into the borders of the wood. Regan was waiting for them there, leaning against a tree with a blissful expression on her face, arms laden with owls and feet surrounded by raccoons. She opened her eyes at the sound of footsteps, straightening, gently shaking her woodland companions away.

"Did you find it?" demanded Cora.

Regan nodded.

They ran on.

At the edge of the wood, where the wall cut the Whitethorn Institute off from the rest of the world, was a deadfall, branches and fallen trees piled together by the wind and the weather until they reached a point almost as high as the wall itself.

"We'll have to jump," said Regan apologetically. "I tried to explain to the stag who led me here that humans aren't that good at jumping, but he didn't understand."

"It's fine," said Cora. "All those laps around the athletic field had to be good for *something*."

"I don't understand," said Miss Lennox.

"He doesn't just take away names," said Sumi, beginning to climb the deadfall. She moved quickly and efficiently, seemingly without fear. "All the doors want is for us to be sure.

They want us to *know* where we belong. This many students, in this small a space, with this many rules and regulations designed to make us miserable? Half of them must know they don't belong here. So where are the doors? They're being kept out, that's where."

"There's no magic in this world," said Emily.

"Of course there's magic. Look at Cora's hair. The magic's smaller, and sometimes it's borrowed, but it's here. The headmaster has magic. He takes names and he somehow keeps the doors at bay, and if you hit the magic number without being sure this world is where you belong, he keeps you on campus, where your door can't ever reach you. Once we break the boundary of the grounds, we'll see what happens then."

"And if no door comes?" asked Stephanie.

"We find a pay phone and I call Eleanor-Elly and tell her she needs to send a bus." Sumi laughed, wild and bright and utterly delighted with herself. "We're leaving. One way or another, we're leaving."

She reached the top of the deadfall and leapt, landing light as a leaf atop the wall. She danced experimentally, then beamed at the group.

"No electricity," she said. "Come on!"

One by one they climbed, even Cora, until Rowena was alone on the ground, looking up at them. The nameless girl waved impatiently.

"Come on," she said. "Come with us."

"No," said Rowena. She grabbed one of the biggest branches from the deadfall and began to yank, trying to pull it free. "Run. All of you, run. Go far, far away, and don't look back."

"Rowena," whispered the nameless girl.

Rowena smiled. It was wavering and small and brave, all at the same time. "Run," she repeated. "Go find your name. Find your door. When you see Bright again, tell her you knew me. Tell her I was cool."

"You were," said the nameless girl.

"Time to go," said Sumi, and the group turned away, sliding down the far side of the wall to land with a thump in the brush on the other side. Sumi was the last to move. She met Rowena's eyes, and nodded, and then she was gone, and Rowena was alone.

She set herself to dismantling the deadfall with all the strength she possessed, ripping it out one branch at a time, making it harder and harder for anyone to follow. When she heard footsteps running through the wood she stopped, looking down at her chapped, torn-up hands, and didn't turn. Whatever was behind her, she didn't want to see.

"Where did they go?" demanded a half-familiar voice. She thought it might be one of the janitors.

"Why do you lock the doors?" Rowena asked.

"This world has magic," he said. "It would have more if it wasn't lured away, carried in the hands of foolish children. We lock the doors and we preserve our natural resources. We keep what's meant to be ours. Where did they go?"

"Away from you," said Rowena. She closed her eyes. "They got away from you."

When his hands landed on her shoulders, she didn't scream. She was proud of that.

Then she wasn't proud of anything at all.

EPILOGUE
GINGERBREAD AND BONE

THE DOOR OPENED OUT of nowhere and disgorged its contents onto the driveway in a pile of limbs and bodies, tangled together like puppies. A short, slightly pudgy teenage girl stepped out last, right onto the bodies of her traveling companions, not seeming to notice when she stepped on their heads or hands. She was dressed in a patchwork vest of countless colors, laced shut with a rope of licorice, over pink leggings that looked to have been knitted out of candy floss. Her hair was pulled into two pigtails and studded with sugar candies. She smiled as she gazed at the house in front of them, which was large and sprawling in the way of homes that had been less "designed" and more simply constructed.

"Is everyone all right?" she asked, before pulling a gumdrop out of her hair and popping it casually into her mouth. "No broken bones?"

"You're standing on my hair," said Cora.

Sumi skipped lightly down from the pile of shifting, groaning bodies, turning to offer her hand to the nearest of them. "We're safe now. Or, if not safe, at least less *un*safe. Eleanor-Elly will be thrilled to meet you all."

Julia Lennox, who had snapped fully back to herself while crossing a gingerbread plain studded with carbonation geysers, pushed herself to her feet. "Even us?" she asked, gesturing to Carrie, who was helping Emily up.

"Even you," said Sumi firmly. "Like you said, years are only numbers. They don't matter here, unless we let them, and I don't think I want to let them anymore."

The nameless girl took Sumi's hand. She was taller now; had grown almost six full inches in the week and a half since they'd fled the school for the forest, and then through the door to Confection that Sumi had seen tangled in a twist of ivy clinging to an old oak. Of the lot of them, her absolute conviction that Confection would never let her go had apparently been the strongest, capable of moving mountains, capable of changing worlds.

Stephanie's door had appeared two days later, in the middle of a forest where the trees had cookies for leaves, spreading so wide they almost blocked out the sun. She'd looked back long enough to shout a quick farewell and then she'd been gone, diving through into a world of lush greenness, the sound of prehistoric reptiles echoing on the wind. The rest of them had kept on walking, kept on searching for something none of them had ever expected to be searching for: a door back to the world where they'd started.

Cora's door hadn't appeared, but her hair was full of rainbows, and she wasn't worried. The Trenches would take her home when it was time.

The nameless girl paused, eyes bright with unshed tears. She looked at Sumi, still holding her hands, and said, "Your door's closing."

"Eh." Sumi shrugged. "I'm not ready to be a wife and a mother and a story for the historians yet, so it's not my time to go back to stay. I know I go home. I can spend a little more time here before that happens."

"Are you all right?" asked Regan, focusing on the nameless girl. "You look like you're going to be sick."

The nameless girl looked at her and smiled, brighter than

it seemed she had ever smiled before. She pulled her hands out of Sumi's and placed them to either side of her own neck, fingers spread, like she was giving herself a hug.

"My name is Marian," she said. "That's my name."

The door of the house banged open as a beautiful boy in a hand-stitched vest burst onto the porch. "Sumi's back!" he yelled. "She's back, and she's got Cora with her!" Kade ran down the porch, cutting across the lawn as several more students piled outside, pointing and yelling. Cora ran toward them, leaving Sumi with the girls from Whitethorn. She and the boy met in the middle of the lawn, wrapping their arms around each other and spinning like pinwheels in the sun. So many things were still broken; so many things still needed to be done. But in that moment, there was victory, and the sound of Marian's joyful sobbing, and a haven to be harbored in.